You shop
you drop

YOU SHOP YOU DROP

C A Shepherd

1

"Gimme a break!" Mark Parlour growled at the radio alarm clock at seven-fifty that Wednesday morning. A pale, narrow hand emerged from under the crumpled blue duvet and slammed down hard on the snooze button for the third time.

"I don't know why you're so grouchy," his wife of twenty-four years commented, squeezing the air from the teat of a baby feeding bottle before stuffing it back in the mouth of a rather cross looking infant. "It's me that was up at Gosh-knows-what hour heating milk for Ro."

Ro was how they affectionately referred to their five month old baby son, the aptly named Rowan – "Little Red One" - with his shock of ginger hair acquired from the paternal gene pool; though, it had to be said, the abbreviation was uttered with considerably less affection in the wee small hours.

"Took me an age to get to sleep last night," Parlour grumbled, staggering out of bed and wrapping a navy silk kimono around his skinny five feet eight frame.

"Brain-ache?" Juliet enquired. Parlour had recently been promoted to Detective Chief Inspector following the untimely death of DCI Brian Sewell in a nasty road traffic accident. Whilst the enhanced professional status and the accompanying rise in salary were most welcome, the added paperwork and politics that the position entailed was proving a considerable drain on Parlour's spiritual well-being. Ditto the arrival of Parlour junior:- a keenly anticipated addition, yet not without a price-tag, with sleep deprivation proving the costliest sacrifice for both Parlours.

"So what's on the agenda for today, then?" Parlour yawned, remembering to show an interest in his wife and child's parallel existence. A secondary school teacher prior to childbirth, Juliet struggled with the loss of self-esteem from which many professional women suffered, on leaving the workplace to care for an infant. Parlour recognised that it was important to bolster her confidence by validating her new lifestyle, however petty and trivial its little routines seemed to him in his less gracious moments.

Juliet groaned. "Need to do a food shop with Junior here. Hopefully he won't do a squitter midway round the Ethnic Cooking Sauces aisle like last time."

Parlour smirked. That was one baby episode he was quite glad to have avoided.

"I expect that will be quite enough for one day, by the time I've put all the shopping away, too," Juliet added, sitting Rowan up on her lap and gently rubbing his back to eject some wind. He obliged some seconds later. For all his little foibles, baby Rowan was pretty good at burping to order. It was a testimony to just what a major upheaval the arrival of a baby represented, that Juliet could envisage one shopping trip filling the entire day. Previously it would have been an hour-long chore, max, sandwiched in between work and the evening meal.

"Thought I might give that new BestCo another go."

Juliet had visited the recently opened store whilst heavily pregnant with Rowan, but had been put off from making a return visit by the crowds of jostling BestCo converts, armed and dangerous with reams of BestCo *BestCard* vouchers.

Parlour exhaled in mock horror. "Consorting with the Great Urban Monstrosity?"

"Yeah, well, needs must," Juliet replied soberly. "We can't keep paying Utopia's prices, even with your promotion, and besides, there'll be a far larger range of baby food at BestCo."

"Thought you were making your own with organic produce from Deverton Farm Store?" Parlour frowned, in that condescending manner of the so-called New Age Man, all sound-bites and no substance. In reality, Parlour was not one of that 21st century breed of flaky new fathers who spoke a good parenting game yet dumped all the drudgy stuff on their wives. All the same, he still displayed a propensity towards pompous affectations on issues of parent-craft which did not bear scrutiny in the harsh light of reality.

"Rowan doesn't like my Sweet Potato Farfalle Bake," Juliet shrugged dispiritedly, "And the Sharon Fruit Surprise came as a bit of a shock to him. But give him a jar of shop-bought *Rigatoni Milanese* and he's in Baby Gastro Heaven. At least it's still organic, even if it *is* in a jar."

"There must be some dodgy ingredient in it," Parlour frowned. "Something that makes babies go ga-ga over it... or should that be goo-goo?"

Juliet shrugged. "Something babies like to chew on, maybe? Extract of dummy or..."

"Crushed remote control?" Parlour grinned.

Juliet laughed.

"I guess it's more important he eats something," Parlour continued in a more serious vein. Inwardly, he made a mental note to decant the contents of the baby food jar into a Tupperware pot, next time they attended the Church Family Lunch. The pc parents' brigade would not approve of processed baby food.

"I guess we're ignoring that advice from the Health Visitor to avoid giving him food till six months?"

Juliet just made a face at him, by which Parlour gathered the subject wasn't even open to debate.

"Yeeuck," Juliet exclaimed, rudely distracted from their discussion as she was splattered with some regurgitated baby milk to accompany the sound effects. "Not another burp with added value!"

"What can I say, you're a natural...." Parlour grinned, debating whether he had time for a shower or not. He'd already got up a full forty minutes later than intended.

"A natural what?" Juliet frowned, but Parlour had disappeared into the en-suite.

The Parlours had met at college in 1983, and Parlour had proposed within the year. A combination of police secondments and Juliet's teaching placements had contrived to keep them apart for a couple of years, but they'd finally made it down the aisle one sunny day in June 1987.

It was nearly eight years since they'd made the move to Deverton. The Parlours had taken advantage of one of those part-exchange deals, and had sold their 1930s three-bed semi in Billock's exclusive Chave area, where Juliet's parents still lived, to *HomeFromHomes,* the popular south coast construction company. In return for their period house, they had received the keys to a spanking new link-detached property on the redbrick Deverton Estate.

The inhabitants of the designer town generally fell into two categories:- young professionals with neither the time nor the aptitude for DIY, in search of an up-together property; or retired couples desperate for a safe haven away from the petty crime and general grime of the city. Deverton offered its inhabitants a chance to start afresh with its newly turfed lawns and made-to-order fittings. And – as Parlour often thought to himself – most of the residents blended in perfectly:- a little bland, but essentially harmless. It was the ideal location for bringing up a young family.

At forty-seven, Mark Parlour had made rapid progress to the rank of Detective Chief Inspector, his ascent up the career ladder accelerated by last year's high-profile arrest of the murderer of Davidson Munroe, leader of the British Alliance of Senior Citizens.

Parlour's surname, allied with a rather unfortunate habit of picking at his skin during moments of stress, had led to the DCI being nicknamed "Pizza" by close friends and colleagues. A late convert to Christianity, Parlour compensated for his religious beliefs with a healthy dash of secular cynicism, accrued through decades in the "wilderness" and a challenging professional life. However, the arrival of little Rowan had caused Parlour to rethink some of his less positive attitudes to life, and at times, to question his whole existence as a DCI. He patrolled some murky waters in his role at Billock CID, that was for sure; in recent months, Parlour had begun to seriously wonder whether he wished to spend the next decade of his life knee deep in the spiritual manure of Hampshire's criminal underworld.

Parlour attended to a particularly vicious spot on his chin, wincing as the antiseptic ointment stung the inflamed area. If only some of the nasty brutes on his patch could be zapped where it hurt.

2

"TIME TO GET UP!" Kat Jankowiczowa bellowed in her native Polish to son, Krzysztof, at a minute after eight that same Wednesday morning. Seven-year old Felicja was already draped over the breakfast table, shovelling a large quantity of Malt Squares into her mouth. She screwed her eyes up, attempting to make head and tail of the small print of a competition on the back of the cereal box.

"Must you eat like a cow?" Kat frowned, laying out her five-year old son's school uniform on the throw-bedecked sofa. The shapeless article of furniture took up the whole of one wall of their pokey two-bedroom flat on the high-rise Billock Towers estate. "You'll get milk down your school jumper again."

"Like they'll care!" the mousy-haired Felicja snorted, throwing her orange juice at the back of her throat like it was a pint of lager on a sweltering summer's day.

"Morning, *Mumia*," Krzysztof greeted his mother, ambling through a moment later. She ruffled his dark hair fondly, shuffling the wannabe Shreddies out of the packet and into his bowl of waiting milk. This had been prepared earlier as part of a series of time-saving rituals concocted by Kat to keep the balls in the air in her work/home-life juggling game.

For six months now, Kat had been working at the brand new BestCo Hypermarket that had invaded a considerable percentage of the green space separating the large urban conurbation of Billock from the outlying borough towns of Deverton and Lexington Green out to the west. There had been no small degree of public outcry at the commercialisation and betonisation of a rare parcel of green land in the area, though almost exclusively by the residents of the outlying towns, keen to maintain the boundary between themselves and the ugly new-town that was Billock.

Nevertheless, despite due consideration having been given and a sympathetic ear lent to both the green vote and the more snobbish protestations of the residents of Deverton *et al*, Foxburgh Borough Council had approved the planning application. In truth, there was a gap in the middle-ground sector of the market. Billock MegaMart, with its dingy orange lighting and oppressive sky-rise shelving, was simply too cheap and nasty for many residents of the town. But on the other hand, few could afford the inflated prices of Deverton's homage to Nigella Lawson, the preposterously titled Utopia, with its home delivery service, E-Topia.

I hope the kids have a better day at school today, Kat thought to herself, furiously rubbing *Herbal Essences* into her long, henna dyed hair as she fitted in a quick shower before the school-run. If the teachers didn't collar her for anything, she'd be out of Eastfield Primary by nine a.m. and on the nine-o-eight bus to the Hypermarket, getting her to work just in time for her 9.30 start.

Kat enjoyed her work at BestCo, especially since she had been taken off shelf-stacking and trained up on the tills. These past few weeks, she'd been asked to do the internet orders, and was enjoying getting around the store a bit more, though the big trolley with its computer console could be rather cumbersome to manoeuvre, especially during peak shopping hours. She was busy, the time flew by, most of the staff were pleasant (though the same could not always be said for the customers) and the pay was good, compared to the pennies she would have earned back in Lodz. Though the children and their various needs usually put pay to overtime, the option was always there to earn more cash for the family, both in England and Poland.

There were quite a few of her compatriots on the tills now at BestCo. Word had spread that Polish women worked hard and complained little – at least at work. Provided that your English was up to scratch, it was reasonably easy to gain employment at the new hypermarket, though the recession was beginning to have some impact on the numbers taken on.

It was through a friend of a friend in the sizeable Billock Polish community that Aleksandra Kowalewa had arrived at BestCo one Monday morning a couple of months ago. The blonde thirty-five year old had soon become best buddies with Kat. Another young mother who'd left Poland for a higher wage packet and enhanced job prospects, Aleks, along with husband Jan and sons Peter and Stanislaw, had been fortunate enough to acquire affordable lodgings soon after arriving in the UK. Altruistic local businessman, Tony Perkiss, had not only given Jan Kowal a job at his light engineering plant; he had also sorted out accommodation for the family, converting a two storey garage on his property into a small house, which he rented out to the couple at a very generous rate. Kat was not *au fait* with all the details, but gathered that a relative of Perkiss had "roomed" alongside some Poles at Buchenwald during the war and the family had maintained a great affinity with the long-suffering Polish nation.

Unlike Aleks, who worked through choice rather than necessity at the newly opened hypermarket, Kat was obliged to work every spare hour she could fit in, by virtue of her husband's relatively low-paid job as a carpet fitter's assistant.

Grygor Jankowicz, it had to be said, rather bucked the trend for efficient, hard-working Poles who put the native workforce to shame. Instead, Jankowicz was Mary to his wife's Martha, preferring to worship at the altar of perceived Western European riches, than work his butt off to put food on the table.

It sometimes seemed grossly unfair to Kat, that she, who was honest and hard-working, should be married to such a low-earning layabout. Had she known at eighteen what she knew now, she would have followed in Aleks' footsteps and married a dull, but diligent worker like Jan, who had plodded along and got himself qualified in work that paid. Instead, she had rushed into marriage, and must suffer the consequences. Grygor may have been far more of a looker than Jan Kowal, but what did a pert bottom and a witty turn of phrase matter once one was saddled with kids, exhausted and struggling to balance the books? Not a jot, as far as Kat could see. It was a dispiriting thought, but quality of life was inexorably allied to financial security.

Differences aside, bringing up children of similar ages and backgrounds in a foreign country provided Kat and Aleks with a special bond that easily overcame the niggling jealousies that Kat harboured towards Aleks at times.

3

"Did you miss the bus?" Kat enquired of Aleks Kowalewa in their native tongue, as Aleks pulled up alongside her with her cart. She was struggling to pin her name badge to her navy jacket, her fingers cold from the outdoors.

"Didn't turn up, did it?" Aleks replied. She clicked a few buttons on her monitor and it flickered into life. "Had to phone Jan at work and get him to run me here. Mr Perkiss won't be too pleased; it's the second time that's happened recently."

"We need to get ourselves a little motor," Kat commented for the umpteenth time in their brief acquaintance. "Take it in turns to drive here. Save all this hassle with bloody British public transport! We could share it - save up between us."

"Whoa!" Aleks interjected, as Kat gathered momentum. "It'll take more than a bit of weekend overtime for you to finance that and I'm not subbing you!"

"It needn't be anything flash," Kat replied, wishing Aleks wouldn't constantly lord her superior financial status over her. "Just one of these little Korean run-arounds. A Kia or a Daihatsu…"

"Please!" Aleks groaned, already converted to British car snobbery. "Anyway, it'd never work…"

"I've heard they're very reliable," Kat countered.

"From a practical point of view, dummy!" Aleks giggled, throwing a loose grape in her trolley at Kat's head. Kat retaliated with an escapee custard cream from hers before a sharp incline of the head from Aleks informed her that the shop-floor manager was heading their way.

"Cut the tomfoolery, you two," Darren Clump frowned at them. "We have a visit from Regional Head Office today, seeing how things are progressing here at BestCo Billock West. I don't want to have to make excuses for any of my staff."

"Yes, Sir," Aleks smiled sweetly, then burst into giggles as soon as he was out of earshot.

"Tom Foolery?" Kat frowned. "Tom Cruise, I know, but not this Tom Foolery man."

"Idiot!" Aleks chuckled, then sobered up as a customer approached her with a query.

"Could you possibly fetch me another trolley?" A lady in her late thirties/early forties enquired archly. "The wheels appear to be moving in opposite directions on this one."

Who do you think I am, the barrow boy? Aleks wanted to reply, but played the subservient customer focus card instead, switching seamlessly into perfect English.

"I'm not supposed to leave my trolley unattended, Madam. Perhaps you could ask one of our in-store Helpers for assistance."

The well-dressed lady cursed under her breath. She was wearing a long camel coat and had a rather formally dressed small daughter in tow, presumably too young to be of school age.

"For God sake, what does one have to do to get a decent service around here?"

Leave God out of it, Aleks nearly retorted, who, being a good Catholic, resented the way the British flung the Almighty disparagingly into every expression of discontent. Instead she smiled apologetically, a gesture born of her own personal code of conduct rather than in reaction to Darren Clump's warning.

The proud woman turned her attention to Kat. "And I suppose you're over here taking British jobs, as well?"

It was a rhetoric question that didn't require an answer, which was just as well, really. Aleks motioned to Kat to hold her tongue, seeing her friend bristle in indignation, about to launch into a diatribe on European employment law and idle British layabouts.

"Now breathe out," she instructed, as the tall woman stalked off, the bewildered child at her side struggling to keep up.

"Stuck up ..." Kat let rip with a string of Polish insult.

"What's with her?" Courtney Brimstock snorted, pulling up next to her two Polish colleagues to pluck some Pink Ladies from the shelf. A pasty young woman with several spare tyres and great wads of flesh protruding from either side of her bra straps, Brimstock summed up to Kat and Aleks everything that was wrong with modern Britain and its unhealthy obsession with cut-price ready meals and cheap fizzy booze.

"A customer just took umbrage with us on account of our nationality," Aleks replied in her best Queen's English, attempting a plummy accent to match.

"Ay?"

"Translate for Courtney, will you, Kat?" Aleks grinned.

"She means a stuck-up cow just got pissed off with us for being in your country," Katerina obliged in the vernacular.

"Tall, long dark hair, little girl with her?" Courtney enquired, removing her waistcoat to reveal damp patches around the armpits of her polyester blouse.

Aleks wrinkled up her nose; it was the worst case of body odour she'd experienced in this country so far. Surely Courtney Brimstock's underarms were far more of an issue for Darren Clump and the BestCo Firing Squad than a flying grape - especially in an environment such as this, where hygiene was paramount.

"That's right – you have come across her?" Kat enquired, raising her head to meet Courtney's gaze, a practice she normally avoided.

"Just asked me to fetch her a trolley - lazy bitch."

"That's the one," Kat confirmed.

"There's a fair few of them come here," Courtney replied. "Think they're too la-di-da for the likes of BestCo. Why don't they bugger off to bloody Deverton to that Stuck-Up-Cow supermarket there, that's what I want to know!"

"Perhaps she is exposing the child to the lower classes, or something," Aleks grinned, keen as ever to put into practice some of the phrases she had learnt at her Advanced English

Conversation course at Billock Adult Ed. "Maybe it's some kind of educational experiment... this is what they call a value ready-meal, *darling*. She probably had that little girl by Caesarean Section as well," she added, labouring over the pronunciation. "*Too posh to push.*"

"Not too posh to push an effin' BestCo trolley, though, is she?" Courtney laughed sardonically, weighing and bagging the apples and plopping them in one of the navy plastic crates on her own trolley.

"Watch out," Kat hissed, "Men in suits. Look busy!"

4

It was ten-forty five by the time Juliet Parlour wheeled her trolley through the doors of BestCo, little Rowan arranged in his baby carrier on top of the metal chariot. He only just fitted into the padded car seat; soon Juliet would have to belt him into one of the child-seats in the trolley itself. She would perhaps need to support him with a cushion to stop him whacking his head on the side of the trolley every time she made a sudden jolt to the left or right.

It was fortunate that such a scenario did not present itself that morning, as Juliet was forced to suddenly wheel the trolley to the right to avoid two members of staff smoking just outside the front entrance to the gigantic supermarket. She wrinkled up her nose in disgust. They appeared to be speaking in another language, something Eastern European by the sounds of it. Not that their ethnicity was a problem, just the social conventions that accompanied it.

Honestly, smoking was bad enough, but right outside the front of a building used by the public, where small babies and expectant mothers could be exposed to the noxious fumes? It was a disgrace. Surely Management could provide a secluded area around the back of the building, if its staff must prevail with this filthy habit? She would be sure to make a comment to the Store Manager. Juliet Parlour was not the first professional mother to require a scratching post once bereft of the cut and thrust of working life.

Her malcontent was soon tempered by the efforts of baby Rowan, who began to blow raspberries and waggle his feet in the air to gain her attention. Attention duly given, the rest of the trip passed relatively smoothly, with no repeats of the unpleasantries of their last foray to the supermarket.

An hour and a half later, Juliet took her place in the queue at Checkout 54, at the far end of the hypermarket, where the tills were not so congested.

18

She could do with shedding a few pounds, Juliet thought to herself, considering the lumpy twenty something wedged into the small area behind her till. Why was it that nearly all the till operators were on the large side, whilst the lads stacking shelves tended to be skinny as rakes? Would it not be far better to get all those porky ladies on the till running round the store fetching and carrying, instead? Or perhaps it was sitting on your backside all day that made you fat? It was one of those curious chicken and egg conundrums, Juliet pondered, pulling her briefs out of her bottom crack, a recent development brought on the accumulation of several pounds of excess bottom baggage. Juliet's weight had ballooned to peak pregnancy levels, now that she no longer had the rigours of breastfeeding to keep it in check.

Britney, Juliet read on her name-badge. Her mouth twitched in amusement at either side. Bet Britney had a really unsexy British surname like *Posthlewaite* or *Ramsbottom*, Juliet thought to herself - rather scathingly, it had to be said. The incongruity of coupling an erstwhile fashionable celebrity forename with a common or garden muck British surname, was a facet of modern society that both irked and amused Juliet in equal proportion.

Mrs Juliet Parlour, Britney snorted to herself, as she swiped Juliet's newly acquired BestCard on the till. *Juliet!* Typical bloody stuck-up cow name. Bet the dribbly little baby was called Oliver or Josh or some other hoity-toity-I-Watch-Jamie-Oliver-and-Usually-Shop-at-Sainsbury name that was deeply unoriginal and not in the least exclusive.

Neither Oliver Nor Josh gurgled contently and cooed loudly. Juliet ruffled his ginger mop, bags now efficiently (if not eco-vantageously) packed for her in several dozen BestCo carriers by an emaciated young lad at the end of the checkout area, skin on his hollow cheeks held together by bulbous purple acne.

You're expecting me to coo with you and comment on how gorgeous your sprog is, but I ain't gonna, lady! Britney thought grimly to herself, handing over Juliet's receipt and money off coupons with a grunt. Juliet scanned the coupons quickly, frowning as she realised they all offered money off items she had just that moment purchased. How irksome – why on earth did supermarkets persist with this infuriating habit?

"Nothing like service with a smile," Juliet said loudly to Rowan as she manoeuvred the heavy trolley away from the checkout. Babies were useful for that, Juliet thought. Those ill-tempered comments she had previously muttered to herself could now be uttered out loud, as she was strictly in company - albeit rather discursively challenged company. Had Juliet turned around at that precise moment, she would have met with an evil glare from Britney Skinner.

5

"Politics Schmolitics," Parlour grumbled, sifting listlessly through an enormous pile of paperwork on his desk that afternoon. With just two days away from the office on a training course, he had managed to accrue one hundred and eighty-seven emails in his inbox. The morning alone had been spent separating the electronic wheat from the chaff and responding to those emails requiring his immediate attention. Now it was time to brave the hard copy stuffed in his top in-tray by Billock CID secretarial support and various members of his team.

"Where's Goodlove got to?" Parlour enquired of his favourite officer, newly promoted Detective Inspector Karen Preece, who had entered his office bearing a cafetière of black coffee.

"Thought this might help you beat the paperwork."

"Cheers, Karen, you're a galaxy of them."

Preece was also Parlour's most competent copper, but whether she was his favourite because she was the most able, or she was more competent as Parlour favoured her and therefore took her into his confidence more, was another of those chicken and egg questions.

"Cam's in the meeting room with the Chief Constable discussing the Lin Dawe business."

Detective Sergeant Goodlove was Billock Police's Gay Liaison Officer. Goodlove had rather publicly outed himself a couple of years back when he had appeared on live national television partaking in the Respect & Tolerance UK fun run in London dressed as the policeman from The Village People! A strapping young man with no effeminate mannerisms of note, it had come as rather a surprise to his colleagues to realise that a gay man had been operating on their force beneath their very noses without anyone even noticing. Marriage and young baby aside, it would have come as far less of a shock to the stereotype driven members of Billock CID had the Fun-Runner in question been DCI Mark Parlour, with his perfectly coiffeured hair, fussy attention to sartorial detail and rather weedy stature.

Lin Dawe, however, was an entirely different kettle of fish. As indiscreet as it was possible to be concerning her sexual preferences, Dawe had got it into her head that she had been overlooked for promotion to Sergeant on account of her gender and sexuality. To make life more awkward for Cameron Goodlove in his capacity as GLO, Dawe had actually applied for that particular post as well, but Goodlove had pipped her to the post.

Parlour groaned. "Not that old chestnut."

"I've heard her called worse."

"That woman needs to brush the chips off her shoulder," Parlour commented, gently pushing the plunger down in the cafetière to avoid the boiling black liquid leaping out of the spout and spilling its grainy load over a memo from the Superintendent. "She lives in a little fantasy world all of her own making, that has no foundation in fact. She's the one living in the dark ages, not us, if she thinks any one of us here would discriminate against her cos she's shacked up with another woman. None of us would dare, in any case! She hears what she wants to hear, exaggerates every little nuance and has the audacity to present it to the Chief as a double discrimination case... there endeth the oratory."

"So why was she passed up for promotion and why did Cam get the GLO post?" Preece enquired.

"Come on, Karen, you know the answers to that," Parlour chided her.

"Just playing Devil's Advocate; you know the Chief's going to get you in there later."

"Police Constable Lin Dawe is not a team player and lets her own prejudices regarding the character and motives of others colour her judgement both in internal matters and in dealings with the public. These deficiencies therefore make her an unsuitable candidate for promotion to Sergeant at this time," Parlour read from his computer screen. "See, already prepared."

Karen grinned then wagged her finger. "He'll want evidence!"

Parlour lifted a brown folder from his desk and thrust it in the air. "Team Building Conference 2007. Official complaint from PC Marian Doyle."

Preece racked her brains. She must have been at that conference, too. Suddenly she clicked her fingers. "Lin had a real go at her across the meeting room about her religious views, right?"

"Called her a Bible-bashing relic from a bygone age, didn't she? All Doyle had done was ask rather politely whether we could all watch our language and cut out the blasphemy wherever possible."

"And Marian Doyle actually lodged a complaint?" Preece asked incredulously. Constable Marian Doyle, like Parlour, had a strong Christian faith, albeit of the Catholic persuasion whereas Parlour was C of E. And like Parlour, she was not one to force-feed it to the rest of the force.

"Yep, and there's plenty more where that came from," Parlour added. "Anyway, that's not my baby, thank goodness. What's new?"

"Nothing of note," Preece replied rather gloomily, keen to get her teeth into a nice juicy murder case again. "The usual drugs and slags and slags on drugs to deal with."

"I'll be reporting you for defamatory comments against *wimmin*, if you don't watch out," Parlour grinned, blue eyes twinkling.

Preece just raised her eyebrows heavenwards and left the room.

***

Baby Rowan's good humour ran out soon after Juliet arrived back at the Parlour home in Deverton.

"Could you just be quiet until I've put the shopping away?" Juliet beseeched the red-faced squalling infant. Rowan was wriggling furiously in his bouncy chair on the kitchen floor, his stomach caving in as he let out another furious screen, little fists clenched in anger.

Juliet brushed the hair from her eyes, attempting in vain not to let Rowan's fury get to her as she haphazardly rammed the tinned goods onto the rotating carousel in her corner unit. It had been a good shopping trip, on the whole, but now she was tired from the effort of lugging the heavy trolley around the busy supermarket and there was still the horrible task of putting it all away left to do.

Juliet let out a large exclamation as she dropped a litre bottle of olive oil on her toe then hobbled over to the kitchen chair. She surveyed the mass of shopping on the floor and her screaming child, then buried her head in her hands.

If you can't beat him – and that was tempting at that precise moment – *then you may as well join him,* Juliet thought to herself, and gave release to the pain and frustration inside.

6

Kat Jankowiczowa flung herself down on the lumpy two-seater sofa in her flat on Floor Fifteen of Billock Towers at five past eight that evening.

"Kids gone down alright?" Her husband Grygor enquired in their native tongue, joining her in front of the television, mug of tea in hand.

"Where's mine?" Kat grumbled.

"I'll make you one in a minute," he replied. "Thought you'd be longer, the mood Kryz was in."

Krzysztof had had a hard day at school, having been placed in the bottom group for reading and being only too aware of the fact, even at the tender age of five.

"We had a good chat. Think I might get Aleks over to help him with his reading and stuff. She understands how they want him to do it, which is more than I do."

Grygor frowned. "Aleks is busy with her own family; perhaps we need to make an appointment with his teacher again."

"But when?" Kat shrugged. "What are the chances of her spare thirty seconds coinciding with ours? Anyway, what do you have against Aleks? You always poo-poo anything involving Aleks, or Jan for that matter."

"Maybe," Grygor demurred. "It's just...."

"Just what?" Kat asked sharply, her eyes meeting his.

"They've landed on their feet, haven't they? With that smart pad of theirs, and Jan's cushy little number at the boss's table. I feel that they rub our noses in it a bit. I don't want them coming *here*.." he gesticulated around the room, "and seeing this."

Kat shrugged. "She already knows where we live."

"All the same..." Grygor's voice trailed off. "Don't you feel that they... you know.."

25

"I suppose she is a bit full of it," Kat agreed slowly. "I hadn't really thought about it before. But she certainly harps on about her kitchen units enough. And as for that English course she's doing at college… guess we're just jealous, huh?"

"Why does it happen for some people, and not others?" Grygor wondered aloud.

Normally Kat would have made a caustic remark about his lack of industry, but tonight she was just too tired and fed up. Instead, Kat just shrugged and got up to make her own tea. It was the first time she had ever seriously queried her lot since leaving her dreary existence in Lodz for the promise of financial reward in the UK. Her limbs suddenly felt heavy with a melancholy that seeped through her pores, as she poured foul tasting water from her cheap value kettle into a chipped china mug. She grabbed her mobile phone from the worktop and impulsively flicked down her contacts list until she found the name she was looking for. Should she?

She looked across the room at her unshaven, greasy haired husband sprawled across the sofa, and thought why the heck not?

Jason Deakin responded to her text immediately.

"Mind if I nip out for a drink with a mate later?" Kat called across to Grygor, trying to keep her tone light and airy.

"If she's paying," Grygor grunted.

That was easy, I didn't even have to lie about his gender, Kat thought to herself, flicking her phone shut. She poured her mug of tea down the sink and wandered through to the bathroom to touch up her make-up and hair. She ought to have a quick shower, but it wouldn't do to arouse any suspicion. You didn't go for the full works if you were just meeting a mate for a quick drink at the local pub.

She'd met Jason during a recent twilight shift on the tills. He'd come to the supermarket at some unearthly hour for a bottle of wine and a pre-packed take-away from the deli counter. Starved of conversation on a particularly quiet evening at BestCo, Kat had flirted with the thirty-something man, who had been dressed in a brightly coloured shirt and a crumpled suit. When Deakin had let slip that he was an Estate Agent at Brentfields in the town centre, Kat had not let on that she lived on the notorious Billock Towers high-rise estate. Neither had she confessed to marriage and motherhood, her ring finger being conveniently covered by the fingerless gloves she wore when passing items through the checkout. This was a habit Kat had taken to recently having cut her palm quite badly on the sharp edge of a bacon packet. There was probably some legal firm that would take BestCo to court for her, but Kat despised the whining blame culture that was drifting eastwards across the Atlantic.

In a ten-minute chat across the conveyor belt, they'd got on like a house on fire, and for some unfathomable reason, Kat had agreed to take his mobile number and call him. The next day, the whole flirty exchange had seemed quite absurd to the normally level-headed Kat; yet still she could not bring herself to delete his number from her contacts list. It was the act of a bored woman, dissatisfied with her lot in life. Katerina Jankowiczowa was living proof that the lawn is not always lusher on the other side.

7

Parlour snapped his small leather bible shut quickly as Karen Preece entered his office at eight fifteen the following morning.

"Sorry, boss, didn't mean to disturb you." Preece was now aware that Parlour liked to start his morning with a quiet ten minutes of prayer and meditation and tried her best to give him space at that point of the day. She didn't expect a young baby afforded him much opportunity for spiritual contemplation.

"It's alright, Karen, I was just about done," Parlour lied, flushing slightly at being caught in the act, so to speak. He looked up and forced out a smile. "So what can I do for you?"

Preece stared at him. Was she imagining it, or was Parlour looking a little moist around the eyes?

"Are you alright, boss?"

"Just a bit worried about Juliet, that's all," Parlour conceded, sensing his face was somewhat of a gateway to his feelings that morning. He knew he should at least attempt to maintain the appropriate emotional distance between himself and a junior colleague but that was easier said than done when Karen Preece knew him so well and could read him, for the most part, like a well-thumbed novel.

"Why? I thought everything was OK," Preece frowned, placing a pile of reports down on Parlour's desk.

Parlour clicked his tongue in exasperation as Preece's action caused the desk to wobble and his coffee to spill.

"Oops, sorry boss," Preece apologised, then blushed as her hand reached for the man-size tissues box at the same time as Parlour's and their fingers grazed together. Her superior seized the box tetchily and mopped up the mess.

"Perhaps I should go..." she demurred and took a step backwards.

28

"No, you're ok. Sit down," Parlour replied, sounding flustered. Preece perched on the chair in the corner and waited patiently as he paced the room.

"She doesn't seem to be very happy, Karen," Parlour admitted finally, his voice cracking slightly. He spread his hands out in an emphatic manner that reminded Preece of Tony Blair. Or perhaps it was more Rory Bremner as Tony Blair.

"I don't know, I thought having this baby meant everything to her, but now Ro's here… she doesn't seem to be enjoying the whole experience very much at all."

"In what way? I thought Rowan was pretty much sleeping through?"

"He's started waking up in the middle of the night again. We reckon he's hungry. We're not supposed to be feeding him solids yet, but we've gone ahead anyway. Now he's filling his nappy in the middle of the night and screaming his head off cos of that!"

Preece made a facial gesture of sympathy but struggled to find the right words. Still footloose and fancy-free at thirty-one, she really had no idea about baby stuff and parenthood, with no elder siblings with offspring to give her an insight, either. Preece tended to turn off whenever other members on the force started on about their babies and kids; now she wished she'd paid more attention, so she could be more use to Parlour. Despite his pernickety nature, she couldn't deny she had a soft spot for him.

"It's not just that," Parlour continued, clasping his hands together in front of him on his desk. "I came home yesterday to find her crashed out on the sofa, with Rowan screeching in his cot and dozens of bags of shopping half put away on the kitchen floor. When she woke up, I asked her if she'd been in long, and she said all afternoon. She'd been shopping in the morning. She'd left those bags there all that time! Some of the stuff was frozen, too – or was."

Preece shrugged. "I've done that many a time, boss. Sometimes something just comes up and you say *sod it*, and do it later. I've been known to waste whole tubs of Ben'n'Jerry's that way."

"It's not like Jules," Parlour shook his head firmly.

"It just sounds like she's shattered, boss. People are too quick to jump to conclusions. Post-natal this and post-natal that. I bet nipper will soon start sleeping through again once his system's got used to the solid food. I think you're reading too much into it."

"I hope so, Karen, I hope so," Parlour said sombrely and stood up. He stretched and looked out of the Perspex window that partitioned his office from the rest of his crime team. "So what's new, pussycat?"

Parlour was all too aware of Karen Preece's – in his view bizarre - penchant for Pontypridd's finest.

"Miaow. There's been a general backlash against Diana Dawe."

"Was there ever a less apt nickname?" Parlour wondered, his brain briefly comparing the voluptuous Ms Dors to the shorn-headed dumpy police constable in question. It was a sure bet nobody ever said it in her presence.

"Gary Cornwallis is thinking of reporting Nico Rossi for racial discrimination. Apparently Rossi called him a Jammy Scouse Bastard for winning the Christmas raffle last year. Cheryl in the Press Office also alleges that Sean Denton groped her bottom in the photocopying room a week past Tuesday; Denton maintains he thought he was reaching into the low wide stationery cupboard."

Parlour chuckled. "You could say they saw a *lin dawe* of opportunity!"

"You're feeling better," Preece grinned, and picked up the top report she had placed on his desk. "And there's this. May or may not be interesting."

"What's that, then?" Parlour frowned, scanning the content of the sheet of A4 handed to him.

"Potential MISPER. Or maybe not. Husband rang us late last night. Gentleman by the name of Robert Girding. Says his wife wasn't at home when he returned from work last night and she's not returned this morning."

"Affair?"

"He says she's not the type, but then they all say that, don't they?"

Preece commented. "You just never can tell..."

"That's a bit harsh, Karen," Parlour chided her. "I can't imagine either Jules or myself *ever* doing that to one another."

"Never say never," Preece said rather flippantly, and left the room.

What did I say that for? She wondered, returning to her desk. Preece turned back to her computer monitor and stared at the screen with exaggerated concentration. This was a technique she often resorted to when feeling flustered. It bought her vital seconds to regain her composure. Bloody hell, she'd come *that* close to giving old Pizza features a hug right then! Was she out of her mind?

Preece reached into her shoulder bag for a small leather diary that was used less for noting appointments than for listing phone numbers and email addresses of the numerous useful acquaintances she made in the course of her work. In an immediate attempt to quash the uncomfortable feelings generated by the encounter with her boss, Preece fished around in her bag for her personal mobile phone and keyed in the number of Shaun Fox, a sexy fellow DI from Thames Valley she'd met at a training day last month. At well over six feet tall, barrel-chested and of African-Caribbean descent (as the current pc jargon would have it), Fox was about as far from Parlour in the looks department as was humanly possible. She'd see if he wanted to meet up for a drink and maybe grab a movie. She was only an hour away from Reading; it wasn't too much of a trek.

8

Robert Girding, Senior Partner at Girding Gift and Davis Solicitors, raked a pale hand through the threadbare remains of a once fine head of thick dark curls, then straddled a weary leg over the side of the king-size bed he ordinarily shared with his wife, Lorraine. He forced his other leg to follow suit and stood up on the cold laminate floor in the bedroom. Whatever had possessed him to replace the luxurious, if a little tired, carpet that had formerly run underfoot, with this clean, yet soulless oak effect flooring? Lorraine, was the answer, he thought wryly to himself:- Lorraine and her desire to please her girl-friends, by supporting their respective husbands in whatever line of trade they happened to be in. Nigel Reynolds Flooring Solutions had a lot to answer for, in his view – though Martin Hill Professional Plumbing was top of his hit-list, given the shocking job Deborah Hill's husband had done in installing the new power shower, managing to crack at least three tiles in the process.

Girding rubbed his eyes, heavy from the early morning slumber to which his aching body had finally succumbed after a night of tossing and turning and pacing the pseudo-wooden floorboards. And then it hit him, winding him like a sucker punch to the stomach:- this was no nightmare, it was reality. Lorraine was missing and the longer she remained missing, the less likely it was she would be found safe and sound.

Girding ambled slowly to the en-suite bathroom and peed in the fashionable white cuboid loo before splashing cold water over his stubbly face. Gawd, he looked absolutely awful, so pale he was almost blue, his eyes pink and bloodshot from lack of sleep.

The phone rang. Girding stood rooted to the spot for a moment, before dashing through to the bedroom to grab the grey cordless BT phone that sat next to his radio alarm clock.

But it was only Billock Police enquiring whether he'd heard from Lorraine. When Girding replied in the negative, the efficient young lady on the other end of the phone informed him they would send a member of CID round later that morning.

At least they don't think she's upped and left me anymore, Girding thought grimly to himself, taking in the implications of this visitation. An intelligent, if rather uninspiring man, Girding was well aware of his shortfalls in the personality department. Yet he remained staunchly faithful to the great institution that was his marriage to Lorraine. They'd been together some fifteen years now, ever since she had first arrived at the Billock solicitors' office where Girding had started his career as a trainee solicitor back in the early nineties. She'd come as temporary secretarial support, but with her clean, classic features and clear diction, Lorraine had soon found full-time employment at the busy Billock firm, and a permanent place at the side of Robert Girding. When Girding fully qualified as a solicitor, and was remunerated accordingly, he predictably proposed to the tall, brunette lady, with her pronounced cheekbones and open visage. Lorraine Wilson accepted and within six months they had tied the knot at the picture-book home church of her parents, in the comatose Hampshire village of Upper Cruddington.

Within five years, Girding had been offered a partnership at Gift and Davis Solicitors. When Gift Senior had retired, to be replaced by his son, Paul, Girding had leapfrogged the plodding Stephen Davis and Gift Junior to become Senior Partner in the firm. It was at this point that the Girdings had moved to their mock Tudor five bed detached in the exclusive Lexington Meadows development, in the village of Lexington Green. Several unsuccessful IVF courses later, with hopes all but dashed of a new generation of Girding solicitors, Lorraine had conceived.

Charlotte Marie was finally born, following a long and painful labour, one June afternoon in 2008. With her mother's classic features and her father's former mop of dark curls, Charlotte soon mutated from a squalling sweaty newborn into a beautiful baby, and was blossoming daily into a gorgeous little girl.

It was therefore with some justification that Robert and Lorraine had created an altar to Charlotte in their living room, with the broad marble fireplace bedecked with photos of Charlotte and her parents at various stages - and in various poses - of mutual adoration. Far too stiff and hemmed in to approve of the modern trend for lolling around on the floor in casual clothes for photo shoots, Robert and Lorraine had opted for traditional family shots, perched on the edge of a velvet two seater with little Charlotte posed alternately on Mummy's or Daddy's lap.

Ever conscious of the need for a single child such as Charlotte to socialise with other children, it was with some reluctance that Lorraine had relinquished her daughter to the local private day nursery three afternoons a week. At first Lorraine had spent the afternoons seeing friends and shopping, but the novelty had soon worn off and Lorraine had started to think about reacquainting herself with the world of work. Advances in modern technology were making it easier than ever to work almost entirely from home and Lorraine found she was able to help out her husband's legal firm by typing out letters and reports dictated by the partners and emailed to her as audio files. These could either be emailed back to the office or Lorraine could drop off the hard copy before picking Charlotte up from nursery at 5pm.

Sometimes Lorraine would pick up Charlotte first so that she could say hi to Daddy in the office. However busy Robert was, he welcomed these visits. He could not help but be proud of his beautiful wife and daughter, both of them head-turners in their own right. Though these parental displays of affection for the child were a little too saccharine for the tastes of most at Girding, Gift & Davis, no-one could deny the obvious depth of Robert's love for both Lorraine and their daughter.

Girding picked up a smaller version of the gigantic print of the three of them that hung downstairs. He kissed his wife in the image then squeezed his eyes shut, uttering up a prayer of desperation to the God he only ordinarily acknowledged when under extreme duress or at funerals. Trauma was a great antidote to agnosticism.

Please just let her be safe, he repeated out loud this time. At least Charlotte was safely at her grandmother's, blissfully unaware of the agony her father was enduring. When the nursery had rung Robert at work to inform him that his wife had neglected to turn up to collect Charlotte that afternoon, and a quick round of calls to the small, but select band of Lorraine's friends had yielded no clues to her whereabouts, Robert had had the good sense to hastily take her to his mother's house in Chave. Lorraine could be stuck in traffic somewhere and could have misplaced her mobile, Robert had reasoned at the time, trying in vain to keep a lid on the panic rising up within. Or more likely, she had ignored his nagging to keep her mobile with her when driving, and not shove it in her handbag in the boot, so that she could contact him in the event of a breakdown or severe delay. It was only when Girding returned to the family home later, that he found her car parked in the garage and her mobile phone on the hall table.

When Lorraine still hadn't made contact by 8pm, their usual supper-time, Robert could not contain his fears anymore. He took out the phone-book and made contact with all the hospitals within half an hour of Lexington Green.

Though he now knew Lorraine's red VW Polo to be sat in the double garage, it was just possible Lorraine had nipped out for a breath of fresh air and been hit by some yobs in a stolen car, or something equally awful. Occupying a geographical location equidistant from two A&E hospitals - Foxburgh

County Hospital and Billock General - a badly injured Lorraine could have been carted off to either. When that yielded no further information, Girding jumped into his staid black BMW and drove slowly around the neighbourhood, meticulously looking up every dark alley and side street, lest he find his wife sprawled unceremoniously in some shrubbery or in the gutter.

It did not occur to Girding just how suspicious his behaviour appeared. It was thus with some degree of shock that he was forced to eject a thirty something Eastern European female from his car. She had slid into the passenger seat of the BMW in the dark lane that ran from the Sun Inn at Lexington Green triangle down to Lovers Lake, a popular location for illicit carnal activity.

But all the time, the clue lay much closer to home. Girding had already checked Lorraine's appointment diary, inside the main compartment of her handbag, located as usual on the telephone table in the hallway. There had been no entries for that day. Yet had Girding taken the simple step of also consulting the calendar hung inside his own kitchen cupboard, he would have discovered the letter "B" entered in biro for the afternoon in question.

9

Mission accomplished, Karen entered National Rail Enquiries into the search engine of her desk PC and looked up evening train times from Billock to Reading. She would have far more fun with Shaun without the bore of having to stay sober for the drive home. Though Preece knew many of her colleagues took the risk, presuming Traffic would turn a blind eye or at worst, let them off with a cheery warning, Preece was not one to risk either sullying her copybook or putting the public at risk. It just took one silly error of judgement and not only was your own career kyboshed, but your whole life and potentially that of others.

Naturally cautious, Preece was averse to any course of action that could cause her regrets in later life, a trait which probably accounted for her single status at the age of thirty-one. She had a good feeling about Shaun Fox, though. Senior in rank and the consummate professional, Fox was a figure she could look up to in all senses of the word, and not just because he towered above her physically. Karen Preece was easily bored, which was probably why a Mark Parlour, with his quick mind and religious zeal, or a Cameron Goodlove, with his sharp sense of humour and alternative lifestyle, proved more attractive to her than the average specimens that were actually available to her. For a while, Karen had wondered whether the attraction of Parlour lay simply in the fact that he was unavailable. But in her heart, she knew there was more to it. But here was Shaun Fox, tall, good-looking, successful and *available*. She really fancied him, which was of some comfort to Karen, who was beginning to worry about her bizarre attraction to the sexually or contractually unattainable of the male species. Seeing Fox might also help her shake off this perverse gravitation towards her skinny, auburn-haired boss. The phone rang, distracting Karen from her reverie. She closed the window down bearing train times and picked up the handset. It was an agitated male voice and within seconds, Karen had identified it as belonging to the solicitor, Robert Girding. She replaced the handset and hot-footed it to Parlour's office.

It was with some reluctance that Karen Preece surrendered the Girding case to DCI Parlour. The emergence of a ransom note turned a potential missing person case into a genuine abduction, with all the associated dark implications.

At just after eleven am, Parlour and his sidekick, Detective Sergeant Cameron Goodlove, rang on the doorbell of Robert Girding's spacious five-bedroom property in Lexington Meadows.

"Just what I expected," Parlour commented, standing back from the stained glass door to survey the front of the house.

"Clearly we're in the wrong profession, Guv," Goodlove grinned, though he couldn't secretly imagine anything worse than sitting in some pokey office pushing paper back and forth all day. It wasn't even as if Robert Girding dealt in nice juicy extra-marital bust-ups; his field was conveyancing work and property wrangles, which was about as dull as it got, as far as Goodlove could make out.

A tall, sallow-faced man with receding black curls answered the door, an expensive smart casual shirt tucked into some unfashionable yet well-cut jeans - *Marks & Spencers* weekend garb, by the looks of it, Parlour thought to himself. He had caught himself drifting into that territory a year or so back, and, in a moment of man-opausal panic, had thrown nearly the entire contents of his wardrobe into a charity bag!

"Good morning, Mr Girding," Parlour stated, extending a narrow, pale-skinned hand. "Detective Chief Inspector Mark Parlour of Billock CID and my colleague, Detective Sergeant Cameron Goodlove."

Parlour didn't think he would ever tire of introducing himself in this way, despite Juliet telling him the novelty would soon wear off. Girding mumbled that they had better come in and they followed him into a rather anaemic cream upholstered living room that apparently served as some kind of gallery of family prints. Parlour noted how tall Girding must be, as he seemed to walk with a permanent stoop, bending his head to enter the living room. Goodlove was well over six feet tall; Girding must have been at least 6'5. *What an inconvenience that must be*, Parlour thought to himself. *You'd think with all his money, he'd get the door frames altered!*

Goodlove rested his posterior on the edge of the sofa, notebook in hand. Parlour wandered over to the bay window and leant back against the sill, folding his arms in front of him. He had a feeling he would appear somewhat weedy and girlish if he perched on the sofa alongside two such well-built men.

"I was expecting the lady detective," Girding stated numbly.

Well, you'll have to make do with the No.1 Man's Detective, Parlour nearly said, but it wasn't an occasion for joshing.

"Your initial call concerning your wife's disappearance came through to DI Karen Preece. I don't really come on board until…" Parlour hesitated.

"Foul play was suspected?" Girding interjected, turning his head to look Parlour briefly in the eye.

Poor chap, Parlour thought to himself. He really looked crushed, physically and emotionally. If Girding himself was involved in his wife's disappearance, then someone should give the man a BAFTA. There was nothing in Robert Girding's beleaguered appearance to suggest he was anything other than a desperate man who'd been up half the night going frantic at his wife's extended no-show.

"You told DI Preece you'd received a ransom note."

"Yes," Girding confirmed dully. "It was hand delivered to my office sometime between closing time and opening up this morning. My secretary found it and rang the police. One of your team bagged it for examination. This is a photocopy."

Parlour nodded, already up to speed on developments. With the slow, exhausted movements of a broken man, Girding reached into his back pocket and retrieved a white sheet of A4, folded in half then half again. Parlour took the letter from Girding and Goodlove immediately strode across to peer over Parlour's shoulder.

Leave £50k in cash in a waterproof bag inside a large Value Cornflakes box next to the electricity substation in Fryer's Dip today at 20.00 hours. Bring the pigs with you and your wife's dead meat.

"Charming!" Parlour muttered.

"Why on earth a Cornflakes box?" Goodlove frowned. Parlour had his suspicions that it involved some sick play on words, but kept his suspicions to himself. It was way too early to start speaking of *cereal* killers.

"And why Value?" Goodlove wondered.

"To disguise the box?" Parlour proffered, though it seemed a rather weak explanation. "Fryer's Dip is that scrubland behind the high-rise council flats in Billock. The Council tried to tart it up as some kind of urban nature haven, and put in a few bird boxes, but it's generally used and abused by fly-tippers - or by the charming residents for walking the pit bulls. A Value Cornflakes box wouldn't look out of place among all that rubbish; probably the sort of people who buy the expensive branded version wouldn't fly-tip behind Billock Towers. At a guess, the ransom collector isn't planning on turning up on the dot at 8pm; he doesn't want to get caught."

"So what do you suggest? I just hand over the money? I can't possibly risk anything happening to Lorraine."

Clearly Girding was devoted to his wife, Parlour thought. There was no question in his mind of putting her life at risk by stuffing the box with Monopoly money or bombarding the area with police surveillance officers. Parlour consulted his watch. It was just after 11 am. Where were they now? Second week in November. The clocks had gone back and so it would be dark by five o'clock. Naturally, they couldn't send any men or equipment in while it was still daylight; that left them with just under six hours to get organised, if they wanted to set up in good time and keep the operation undercover.

"We can't let you go in there alone," Parlour said eventually. "I reckon we have a couple of plain-clothed officers lurking in the area, carrying out some activity that's not out of place in the surroundings."

"What, shooting up?" Goodlove chortled. Parlour glared at him. He had hoped Goodlove would have grown out of flippant comments at inappropriate moments by now. That was Sean Denton's domain.

"I was thinking more of dog walkers or twitchers," Parlour stated.

"Ha ha, sure Denton will be up for a spot of bird-watching," Goodlove chuckled, who just couldn't resist the temptation.

"Isn't it risky?" Girding frowned. "I can't possibly have Lorraine's life placed in danger. I would never forgive myself if anything happened to her – and neither would Charlotte."

Personally Parlour felt Charlotte was probably too young to apportion blame in this way, but concurred that it would be tragic for the infant to lose her mother.

"We don't know how dangerous these people are," Parlour stated. "They could be novices after a quick buck - kids from the tower block after drug money – though their spelling's too good for that. Or some kind of mavericks with a warped sense of humour, hence the Value Cornflakes box. Or they could be hardened criminals with no respect for human life. We just don't know. We certainly haven't come across them at Billock CID."

"Let's hope it's the former," Girding replied soberly.

"You told our DI last night that Lorraine's car was still in the garage," Parlour stated.

Girding nodded. "Her handbag's on the telephone table, too. She must have nipped out for some fresh air."

"Is she in the habit of going for a walk?" Goodlove enquired. Girding frowned. "Not really. I mean, she'd pop out for a reason, like to buy the paper or some milk. But her purse is in the handbag."

"Might she have stuffed a fiver in her pocket, if she was just popping out to the One Stop?" Goodlove wondered.

"Not her style, really," Girding replied, shaking his head slowly.

"Lorraine's…a lady. She always goes out with her handbag, make-up on, not a hair out of place. She wouldn't just stuff her mobile and some cash in her pocket and rush out quickly like a chap would."

Like Juliet, Parlour thought to himself, smiling in spite of himself, imagining his wife stuffing her arms into that awful biker jacket of hers and scuffing down the hill to the convenience store in a pair of scruffy mules, a couple of loose coins jangling in her inside pocket.

"So her mobile's in her bag, too?" Goodlove queried.

Girding nodded. "It's in the hallway, check it out if you like. There are no relevant messages on the voicemail; I checked. And Lorraine doesn't *text*."

Girding said the word with derision in his voice.

Damn, Parlour cursed inwardly. He had been hoping Lorraine's mobile phone would have yielded a clue. Still, it would have been the easiest thing in the world for Girding to have wiped some messages, but records from the mobile phone company could be accessed without too much trouble in a case such as this.

He would need to delve deeper into Girding's character... there was a sense in which Girding was just too grey and unassuming to be true. Perhaps someone held a grudge against him and abducting his prize asset was one sure means of extracting revenge. Parlour mused on such matters as Goodlove took full details of the events leading up Mrs Girding's disappearance.

"I know you've been through this already with Detective Inspector Preece, but you're sure you've contacted all family and friends?" Parlour double-checked once Goodlove had completed his notes. "Yes. Nobody's seen her nor heard from her bar the usual weekend phone calls from her parents."

Goodlove consulted his pocket book. "You also told our DI that there were no appointments in her diary."

"No, it looks like she'd kept the afternoon free for housework. She sometimes does bits and pieces on the computer for the firm, just secretarial stuff. But we've had a quiet week and I had nothing for her. She's changed the sheets in Charlotte's cot-bed; the dirty ones are in the washing machine. Charlotte's nappy had leaked a little yesterday morning, I offered to change the bed, but Lorraine said she'd do it in the afternoon as she was planning on "blitzing the house" as she put it."

Girding looked wistful as he recalled his wife's last words to him the previous morning.

"Don't you have a cleaner?" Parlour enquired, eyebrows furrowing. It was unusual for a couple of their financial status not to have some form of domestic help these days.

"We do, but she's on compassionate leave at the moment. Her mother died of stomach cancer very suddenly a couple of weeks back. Not long after diagnosis - tragic really," Girding stated dully, in the manner of one who had repeated the information too often to muster up the requisite emotion demanded of him, an effect compounded by the terrible predicament closer to home in which he currently found himself.

"It's often the way with stomach cancer," Parlour nodded, whose aunt had succumbed in a similar fashion a few years back.

"Do you think she was dragged off in a car then?" Girding enquired.

Parlour made a dubious face. "I'd say it was more likely someone called at the door. We need to check for tyre imprints on the gravel outside – she may have arranged for someone to call round and neglected to mention it to you. Perhaps it seemed too insignificant to her, but it may prove vitally important to our investigations. And now we know for sure that she's been abducted, I need to send some officers round to conduct further investigations. I hope that's alright with you?"

Girding spread his hands out in front of him. "Whatever you think best, Detective Chief Inspector. I haven't a clue what could have happened to her, please do whatever you need to do. I've nothing to hide. I don't want Lorraine to suffer for a moment longer than she has to."

"I'll need to question the neighbours, to see if anyone saw her go out for a walk, or saw anyone call at the door. I'll get some officers on door to doors in the surrounding area, too," Parlour stated.

"Fine, but you'll find there's no-one around in the Close through the day," Girding commented. "The only non-working couple are the Jacobsens at number four, who've retired. But they're away in Italy at the moment. They have a time-share on the Adriatic, lucky sods."

"All the same, we'll do some door-knocking. You never know, someone might have been off work sick or something," Parlour replied. "Meanwhile, I'll arrange for two of our specialist surveillance officers to head to Fryer's Dip at dusk."

"So I need to get £50k of my own money out the bank then?" Girding confirmed.

"Unfortunately, we don't have a large stash of fake banknotes at Billock CID, no," Parlour shook his head, kindly. "Do you anticipate a problem with that?"

"The bank should authorise that," Girding stated, with the confidence of a man with six figures in the bank.

"I'll need the serial numbers on the banknotes," Parlour reminded him.

Girding looked blank.

"To track the movement of the notes, if need be," Parlour explained patiently. "We'll put tracking devices in the bag, but they can fail – or get destroyed."

Girding nodded despondently.

"Anyway, get the bank to give me a call if they do have an issue with it," Parlour continued. "I'll get some plain-clothed officers to hang around in Lexington Green near the bank, in case you're being followed. And I'll get one of our constables to get you a box of cheapo Cornflakes."

Girding shuddered. "Do you think the kidnappers know you're here now? What if they harm Lorraine because I called you to the house?"

"The note indicated she'd be harmed if they saw us at the ransom handover point," Parlour replied, attempting to reassure him. "They can't expect you not to call the police when your wife has disappeared. They knew you wouldn't get that ransom note until the morning if they put it through the door outside office hours – you'd hardly wait that long to report your own wife missing."

"I suppose," Girding replied shakily.

"This is bonkers," Goodlove stated, shaking his head, and snapped his pocketbook shut. He rose to his full height and stretched, nearly taking out a gigantic chandelier in the process. He did not have a good feeling about this case; something told him the outlandish ransom note was a smokescreen for an altogether more sinister affair.

10

"You're quiet today – is everything OK?" Aleks Kowalewa enquired of her colleague as they got on the number thirty-eight bus to Billock West Superstores.

"Just tired," Kat replied, checking her mobile phone for texts or missed calls, a nervous habit that drove her husband and children mad.

"Late night?"

"Mmm."

"Lucky you!" Aleks groaned, whose husband had been too tired for any bedtime action for weeks on end now. When your boss had given you a well-paid job and provided a roof over your head, you could hardly refuse a bit of overtime. Tony Perkiss had Jan Kowal over a barrel, and Aleks was paying the price – at least in the bedroom department.

"As if!" Kat snorted in derision.

"Is there something you're not telling me?" Aleks enquired, eyes wide open as she inclined her head conspiratorially towards her friend's.

"I just couldn't get to sleep, that's all," Kat replied, which wasn't a lie, her head spinning following her illicit rendezvous with the local estate agent.

Aleks wasn't convinced but sensed the topic wasn't open to further debate so changed the subject to the new shift pattern at BestCo. She'd have another bash later.

In truth, Kat felt very uneasy about the previous evening. Essentially an honest, up front kind of person, it was the first time Kat had gone behind Grygor's back in this way. Even now, she wasn't quite sure what had come over her. She had just felt so trapped and desperate last night, the gloomy flat and her increasingly down-at-heel husband driving her out into the dark, cold night in search of some sparkle. She had returned home on the number three bus feeling worse than ever, however. It soon became clear that Jason Deakin had only one thing in mind, and it wasn't discussing recent trends in the property market. Within half an hour of them meeting in a city centre pub, Deakin had announced that he had the keys to any number of vacant properties where he could show Kat a good time. Kat blinked back tears of shame as the bus rumbled towards her place of work and Aleks griped on about work matters. Clearly Deakin had thought she was some piece of Eastern European slack, desperate for a bit of rough and tumble; he'd all but slapped a fifty quid note on the table next to her G&T. When it became apparent that she was *not* going to accompany him back to Brentfields' premises for the keys to the nearest vacant shag pad, he'd made some excuse about needing to be up early in the morning. Deakin had left her alone in the noisy chain pub, with only a couple of dozen spotty students and Sky Sports for company.

Fortunately Grygor had been fast asleep on the sofa when she had returned just after eleven pm, snoring alarmingly in front of a cheap and nasty film on one of the less reputable television channels. Kat had left him there, keen to avoid any awkward questions. He would have forgotten all about her little foray into the night, by the time they met again over supper the following evening. With a bit of luck, she'd never clap eyes on Jason Deakin again and it'd all be forgotten in the blink of an eye.

***

"What are you looking so pleased about?" Parlour enquired of Karen Preece, returning to his office just after midday.

"The sun's out," Preece replied rather unconvincingly, thinking just how twee and unmanly Parlour was with his naff little square sandwiches and his plastic bowl of chopped sweet salad. "How was Robert Girding?"

"Shell-shocked," Parlour replied, pouring himself a black coffee from a freshly brewed cafetière.

"No idea where she could have got to, then?"

"Reckons she's not the type to go out for a walk just for the fun of it, and certainly not without her twinset and pearls."

"Think he's hiding anything?" Preece enquired.

"Nope," Parlour shook his head. "Seems a genuine enough fella. Boring and devoted to his wife and kid."

Don't the two go hand in hand, Preece thought silently to herself. "Think she just got bored and did a runner?"

"What, and left the child behind, a child that took years to conceive?" Parlour looked highly dubious.

"Maybe she reckoned this motherhood lark wasn't all it was cracked up to be. Maybe she had post-natal depression or something."

Parlour just looked at Preece, who blushed and looked away. She hadn't meant to sound so insensitive.

"There's a ransom note, remember? No, I think she was abducted very close to her house, if not *from* her house," Parlour continued after an awkward pause. "Her car's in the garage, her handbag's still in the hallway complete with purse and mobile phone. Her diary's also in the bag with no appointments listed for that afternoon. Either she was the victim of a ruse and dashed out the door to help someone allegedly in distress, or someone called at the door and forced her into a vehicle. That's my guess."

"Or she vanished without a trace deliberately, taking no personal items with her," Preece added, "and concocted a ransom note to deflect suspicion."

Parlour shook his head.

Preece shrugged. "Just considering all the options."

"I suppose we can't rule out she's got tired of her husband. He's not the most dynamic chap in the world, I grant you that. You *could* fake your own disappearance. But the proof will be in whether someone turns up and takes the money. And following that line of thought, I suppose we should check that the daughter is safe, too. If Lorraine Girding has left of her own accord, she may well come back for the child. I expect she has a set of keys for her parents' house; she could sneak in and take the little girl when she was sleeping. However, I find the whole scenario highly unlikely. She seems well set up with Girding - house, child, cushy little part-time job working from home."

"I agree, but I wouldn't rule out a lover - or sheer boredom," Preece stated. "She could easily have another PAYG mobile in another handbag and a stash of banknotes. She wouldn't take her own car with her if she was trying to run away, would she, so that could be a red herring."

"Red Polo, actually," Parlour grinned. It was a feeble joke best ignored, and Preece duly obliged.

"I suppose she could have had a hire car parked up around the corner – it's worth a check," Preece persisted. "You can think you want something, then when you have it – bam! - there's nothing left to strive for. I wouldn't rule it out, that's all, that Lorraine Girding's simply had enough of the cushy life."

"Maybe," Parlour murmured in reply, momentarily lost in reverie. But he soon snapped out of it – had to, in the circumstances. He hastily drained his mug of coffee and stood up straight. "Can't stand around here chatting. Need to organise a surveillance unit for tonight."

***

If he dares complain about the phone bill, Juliet Parlour thought gamely to herself, taking some Rich Tea biscuits from the tin to dunk in her coffee, *I shall say it was all his idea, to phone a friend.*

The Parlours had sat up talking late into the night, unable to get back to sleep following a colicky wake-up call from baby

Rowan. Parlour had discussed the sheer volume of paperwork suffocating him, preventing him from focussing all his attention on the demands of a puzzling new case. Juliet had admitted that life with a baby was not all it was cracked up to be, thereby confirming Parlour's fears that his wife was suffering from some form of depression. It was probably a combination of swirling post-partum hormones and tiredness, Parlour thought. And tied in with that, the loss of self-worth that must inevitably accompany swapping the identity of Juliet Parlour, Head of Year 9 at Billock Community School, for Juliet Parlour, Mother-of-One and full-time milkmaid. His advice to his wife was to phone a friend. And taking the *Millionaire* analogy one step further, to choose a friend who might have the right answers.

So Juliet had settled on Kate D'Archeville, an old friend from teacher training college, now based in Wiltshire, who had taken a career break a couple of years back to bring up her twin girls, Ludmilla and Acacia.

Hearing the relief in Juliet's voice when she had picked up the receiver, Kate had set the girls up in front of a Muzzy DVD, sensing this was no five minute call.

"So what's up?" Kate enquired in a kindly tone of voice, once both women were settled at their respective ends of the phone and news of husbands duly swapped. "I'm guessing you're after some baby advice – not how to teach Key stage 3 English to a bunch of spotty teenage Nintendo nerds?"

"How did you guess?" Juliet groaned.

"Because I'm the only one of your *coterie* so far, besides yourself, to have signed up for the Financial Suicide Club that is parenthood?"

Juliet chuckled, though not without a seam of wistfulness in her tone. "If only money were the issue."

"What's up, got the baby blues?" Kate enquired, more gently this time. Juliet croaked out a yes before dissolving into tears.

An hour later, armed with lots of good tips on how to look after herself and get some much-needed *Jules-Time*, Juliet turned on the computer and located a popular on-line grocery website. Time to let someone else do the hard graft.

<h1 style="text-align:center">11</h1>

Shortly before 5pm that evening, DC Sean Denton and DC Leanne Quinn sat in the back of an innocuous white van used by Billock Police for surveillance work, a mile to the west of Fryer's Dip and well out of sight of Billock Towers.

"Are you clear on your brief?" DS Goodlove checked with them from the front seat, himself dressed down in an old paint-stained sweatshirt and ripped jeans he'd worn that weekend to help decorate a mate's flat. Parlour, with his enhanced media profile and distinctive red hair, had elected to stay at the station and communicate with Goodlove by telephone, rather than risk exposing the operation. Despite his desire to be at the forefront of the action, Parlour had to accept a more deskbound role as Senior Investigating Officer on the case, assessing incoming intelligence and delegating donkey work as appropriate.

"We walk towards Fryer's Dip with the Rotts," Denton stated, referring to the stocky Rottweilers they had borrowed from the private collection of Paul the police dog handler. They would need to keep their distance from the ransom point, in case the appearance of the fearsome hounds acted as a deterrent to the ransom collector. It was hoped that the use of Rottweilers rather than Alsatians would not suggest a police presence. Parlour had initially felt smaller dogs would deflect suspicion away from them, but decided that Rottweilers were far more in keeping with the hardened image of the housing estate bordering Fryer's Dip than some dainty little pooches.

"We act as if we're more than just friends, possibly lovers using dogs as an excuse for being out together," Leanne Quinn continued. "There's lots of stopping for face to face chats, hand holding, quick cuddles, general canoodling."

Denton snickered. "Then I get you up against a tree and…"

"Whoa! Down boy!" Goodlove interjected, grinning.

"I keep looking at my watch, giving the impression time is short and I have a husband to get back to," Quinn added, who was taking the task altogether more seriously.

"Won't it look like we're undercover police officers wondering how close it is to 8 o'clock if we do that?" Denton frowned.

"Maybe…" Goodlove nodded. "OK, scrap that bit. Just make sure you're well back from the electricity substation, far enough back that the kidnapper feels he can discretely snatch the box away but close enough for Sean to follow him."

"And I get left babysitting the mutts?" Quinn groaned, who was no dog lover.

"I'd say a clear case of sex discrimination," Denton grinned.

"Don't even go there!" Goodlove groaned, holding his hand up in protest. He'd just about had as much as he could bear of Lin Dawe that week. "Now, you've got your stab vests on?"

Both nodded in confirmation.

"Right. You can get going, then. Do nothing to arouse suspicion. No communication with anyone until the ransom collector is at the point of taking the money. I expect he or she will pause to check the contents of the box and will probably remove the bag of money. That's when you start to pursue him – without his... or her... finding out. Girding should arrive a minute or two before eight to place the box there. Ignore him totally. You only have eyes for one another, remember."

"I am *so* glad this is a one off," Denton grinned, blowing kisses at Quinn.

"Would you like me to walk the dogs with you instead, then, Denton?" Goodlove grinned.

Denton scrambled hastily out of the van.

***

At 7.58, as arranged, an ashen-faced Robert Girding placed a large Value Cornflakes packet stuffed with banknotes at the base of the electricity substation box in the wet and muddy centre of Fryer's Dip. When nobody had arrived to take the box by nine pm, Denton and Quinn returned to the white van, the redundant dogs plodding along dispiritedly beside them, lest they arouse suspicion. Nobody would walk their dogs in that miserable plot of land for longer than an hour, however side-tracked they may be by romantic aspirations. It could well be the case, anyway, that the abductors were staying away until the coast was completely clear.

Goodlove kept his eye on the pictures relayed back to the van via a wireless CCTV camera that had been discretely attached to a tree earlier that afternoon. But there was no sign of a ransom collector.

"Do you think it's a hoax, Cam?" Denton enquired, who would never have dared address DCI Parlour in such familiar terms.

"Not sure," Goodlove conceded, keeping his eye on the video screen with its eerie green night-lit footage. "Could just be someone trying to put the wind up Girding, maybe someone with a grudge against him - but his wife's still missing. Or maybe they've spotted us. You'd think they'd at least come and get the money though. Still, the night is young."

Quinn groaned. "Please don't say we have to remain holed up here all night. It's perishing and I'm famished, too! It's been a long day."

DCI Parlour would have intervened at this point with a caustic remark on commitment and duty to the public, but Goodlove was far more easy-going than his senior officer.

"I'll radio for an unmarked car to collect us all; the night boys can relieve us," Goodlove replied.

***

Still recovering from a late night out with friends, PC Jordie Mitchell had nodded off at intervals during the night watch,

55

relying on her colleague, PC Jamie Rushton, to keep an eagle eye on Fryer's Dip. Unfortunately, Constable Rushton was in the throes of an intense romantic entanglement and was too busy texting his latest squeeze to concentrate on the CCTV footage on his screen. Had either been attentive to the pictures relayed from the scrubland to the unmarked van, they would have spotted a motorcyclist in dark clothing enter Fryer's Dip from the east. And had Constable Rushton not ambled around outside to enjoy a cigarette while PC Mitchell dozed on, he would have heard the motion detector bleep as the motorcyclist grabbed the package near the substation before zooming off into the night.

12

"Can someone please explain to me how not one, but two, trained officers can fail to spot a motorcyclist riding through Fryer's Dip flashing red on a heat-sensitive camera?" Parlour yelled in an uncharacteristic loss of temper the following morning. "And don't tell me the motion alarm wasn't working – we tested the equipment thoroughly beforehand!"

PC Mitchell stared at the ground morosely, whilst Rushton stared at a point somewhere to the east of Parlour's face, avoiding his furious expression. Parlour banged the desk at the front of the incident room with his fist.

"All you were asked to do last night was focus on one thing, *one thing*, and you couldn't even manage that. Now we've precious little chance of tracing this motorcyclist and Robert Girding has lost £50k. *And*, more worryingly, there's neither sight nor sound of Mrs Girding!"

"Sir, we've got officers scouring the area for an abandoned motorcycle," Goodlove interjected feebly, "and searching the A-road for tyre traces. We've paused the picture and we have a fair idea of the make and model of the bike. Unfortunately, the number plate is obscured by mud."

Parlour flapped his hand in a derisory gesture and left the room.

Goodlove took a deep breath then exhaled, emitting a long, low whistle that sounded like the wind in the trees, an appropriate metaphor in the circumstances. Causing little more than a ripple in the undergrowth, the kidnapper or accomplice had made off with fifty thousand pounds in a Cornflakes box. The tracking device had failed and so far the banknotes remained untraced.

The call they were all dreading, admittedly more for its professional implications than on compassionate grounds, came through just after the two minutes silence for Remembrance Day. It was radioed in by Police Constable Leah Bridgeport, who had taken over the morning shift stationed at Girding's house. Girding himself was too distraught to even formulate a word, let alone pick up the telephone.

Parlour had made sure the house itself was guarded, in the vain hope that the abductor, or a member of their gang, would turn up with further communications. Unfortunately, manpower issues prevented Parlour from placing an additional officer at Girding's office, where the original ransom note had been pushed through the door. This was a great shame, as the second communication from the kidnappers was lying on the hallway carpet of Girding Gift and Davis when the administrator, Lisa Footwell, arrived at work at just before 8.30 am that morning. The white windowed envelope, marked Mr Robert Girding, Private and Confidential in typescript, was just one of several hand-delivered letters addressed to the partners, a quite normal occurrence at the busy local firm of solicitors. Lisa had placed them on her desk along with the post that had arrived just after 9am; she had been too busy fending off a barrage of phone-calls to do anything with the letter in question. As Girding was obviously not going to make an appearance in the office that day, Lisa had put the innocuous white envelope to one side for the time being.

As she busied herself making teas and coffees for the solicitors in between answering the switchboard, Lisa Footwell forgot all about the instruction from DCI Parlour to keep an eagle-eye on the incoming post. It was only when Girding's colleague, Paul Gift, gathered all the staff together in his office to impart the shocking news that Lorraine Girding had been kidnapped, that Lisa had recalled the hand-delivered envelope marked "Private and Confidential." Paul Gift had immediately requested to see the letter and had the fortitude to wait until he was alone to open it – which was just as well in the circumstances.

Parlour himself had turned up within the half hour, DC Sean Denton in tow.

Sweat lined Parlour's forehead and the palms of his surgically gloved pale hands, as he considered the communication before him in the privacy of Paul Gift's office. Typed on one sheet of A4 was the terrifying message:- *Better not involve the Pigs next time we strike, or Lorraine Girding really will be dead meat.*

Below the ominous warning, the abductors had copied a print of a gagged and bound Mrs Girding, propped up against a wall of what appeared to be some kind of darkened outhouse, perhaps a garage or storage container. The expression on her face was obscured by a bad case of red-eye, but the skin tone and the position of her body suggested she was still alive – at least at the point of taking the photo. There was nothing to suggest that she was injured in any way.

"Sure that's her?" Denton enquired hopefully.

Parlour nodded sombrely. "Fairly sure, we'll need to show it to Girding, of course. At least she seems alive, though I'll need a Forensics expert to take a look at the picture. And of course, there's no way of knowing what's happened since the picture was taken. Shame it's not a real photo - a lot of the definition is lost in this. And there's no date-stamp on it either."

He looked at the letter again. It appeared to be printed on the same value white copier paper as last time, as the sheet was slightly wrinkled from the weight of the colour ink in the photo insert. The same largish Times New Roman font had also been selected as last time. Gift's fingerprints would be all over the communication; it was a shame he had not thought to wait for a police officer to arrive before checking its contents.

"Done on the same home printer as the ransom note, by the looks of it," he commented to Gift and Denton. "We'll get it sent off for prints - there may be some faint greasy fingerprints on the paper, and I'd like it confirmed that Lorraine Girding is alive in the photo, as far as can be ascertained from something of this quality. Next time, would it be possible to wait before opening any suspicious mail items, Mr Gift? We need to keep it all potential evidence as print-free as possible."

Gift held his hands up in apology.

"One thing's for certain, though," Parlour continued.

"What's that?" Gift and Denton enquired, almost in unison.

"This is no prankster." Parlour looked up at Denton then across the table at Paul Gift.

"Do you know what bothers me more, though I wouldn't have said it in front of Gift?" Parlour commented to Denton, once they had returned to the car.

"That there's going to be a next victim?" Denton asked soberly. Parlour nodded gravely.

"Hopefully it's just a ruse," Parlour stated, with absolutely no conviction in his voice. The chilling follow-up note coupled with the image of Lorraine Girding bound and gagged in a dark outhouse had taken away any lingering hopes that this was simply the work of some youthful miscreant trying to raise some quick cash. Parlour kicked the front tyre in disgust.

"Take heart, Sir," Denton called to him, starting up the engine. "At least she's not dead."

"Come on Sean," Parlour chided him. "Don't be so naive. That photo could have been taken before they killed her."

It was a sobering thought, and the two men sat in silence for the duration of the journey.

13

Parlour was not in the least bit surprised to arrive back at Billock CID to find a summons from the Superintendent on his desk. He sighed. What a nightmare; a botched surveillance operation and a missing woman - both on his patch, and both under his jurisdiction. Parlour picked up his A4 notebook and made himself a strong cup of black coffee. Thermal mug in hand, he headed along the corridor to the Superintendent's office. It was sure to be a long one.

****

Juliet hastily flipped the lid down on her laptop as she heard the key turn in the lock at seven twenty-eight that evening. She had all but completed her first on-line grocery shop, though it had taken considerably longer than anticipated. Kate had warned her that it took ages the first time, but thereafter the process became much simpler, as you could simply repeat last week's order, adding and subtracting items to and from your original list as appropriate. Juliet had briefly toyed with the idea of using E-topia, the online grocery service of Utopia, the local upmarket store in Deverton. It would look considerably better for one of their classy claret vans to pull up outside their house in Spatchcock Drive next Wednesday, than a lower-middle-class BestCo van. But the off-peak delivery charge of seven pounds forty-nine was prohibitive. And besides, it seemed that they had precious few delivery slots and limited coverage in the area, despite the existence of its flagship store in Deverton.

Mark would undoubtedly think she was being a ninny, wasting even four pounds getting the shopping delivered, instead of visiting the store in person. Some things were better left unmentioned, Juliet decided. Whilst in principle, she was of the view that one should not keep secrets from one's spouse, there were times when it was simply more practical to do so, to avoid unnecessary stress and friction. So long as he found what he wanted in the cupboards with the BestCo logo on it, why should Mark suspect a thing? The name BestCo Billock West would appear on the Credit Card bill as usual, delivered or not – she'd checked that out with Kate first. Anyway, it wasn't as if she had committed a crime, was it? He would be so happy in a few weeks, when he saw for himself how much less stressed out she was, that he would surely write off the four pound delivery charge as being a small price to pay for his wife's happiness. Or at least, this was how Juliet justified concealing the truth from her husband for the time being.

"Ro asleep?" Parlour enquired, as Juliet effected a casual stroll into the kitchen and planted a kiss on her husband's mouth. Parlour squeezed his wife's rather overgrown bottom.

"Mm," Juliet replied, tutting as she hung up Parlour's coat for him in the hallway. "Had an easier afternoon," she explained, omitting to mention her forays on the BestCo website. "Ro had an early tea at four and has been asleep since."

"So he'll be up at midnight then?" Parlour frowned.

"You can't have it both ways," Juliet snapped.

"What do you mean?"

"Tell me to look after myself, take it easy, then grumble when I let him sleep early to get some *me*-time."

Parlour took a deep breath and stopped himself firing back a retort concerning the lack of z-time he would undoubtedly endure later.

"I can't guarantee I'll be here later, Jules," he said in a measured tone, instead. "We've heard from the kidnappers of Lorraine Girding. They sent a photo of her in some kind of lock-up, but they could have killed her by now, of course."

Parlour trusted his wife implicitly to keep such insider information to herself.

"But she looks alive in the photograph?" Juliet checked, distracted from her domestic situation for once.

"It's only a photocopy, but yes."

"So why are they holding onto her – assuming they are? Have they demanded more cash from her husband?"

"It's worse," Parlour replied soberly. "They appear to be using her as bait. They say they'll kill her if the police are involved *next time*. Of course, it could be a load of phooey and she's already dead."

"Next time?" Juliet echoed.

Parlour nodded grimly. "We should have taken the kidnappers' warning more seriously. I thought we were discreet enough with the surveillance op, but obviously not."

Parlour shook his head and looked up at his wife. "I'm in deep doo-doo at the moment, Jules. The Super's spitting blood, I've just *got* to get some leads on this."

"So they're planning to strike again... oh boy," Juliet shuddered, leaning back on the kitchen worktop.

"So they say - those were the words they used, in fact," Parlour nodded. "So far our kidnappers have got away with £50k, we're none the wiser where Lorraine Girding's being held and it looks like they're planning another abduction. And if we set up another surveillance operation, Mrs Girding could die, if she hasn't already. They've got us over a barrel; it's a complete nightmare. No wonder the Super's getting tetchy."

"So you have no idea whatsoever who's taken her or where she's being held?" Juliet recapped.

"None whatsoever. And the dolts on the overnight watch missed the motorcyclist who grabbed the booty."

"Hardly your fault," Juliet countered.

"My team," Parlour shrugged. "And I have to blame myself for not taking the threat seriously concerning police involvement."

"But you tried your best to keep the surveillance operation secret, and how would Girding have reacted if it *had* all been a hoax and he'd lost £50k?"

"Your loyalty is touching, Jules," Parlour smiled wanly, kissing his wife on the head. "But misplaced on this occasion. The safety of Lorraine Girding, the sanctity of human life, should have been paramount in my mind."

"Did you bug the banknotes?"

"We put several tracking devices in the cereal box and in the actual bag of cash, yes, but they failed."

"But they might track down the banknotes - I guess you put a warning out?"

"That's always a long shot, Jules," Parlour replied gloomily.

"I think you're being too hard on yourself," Juliet frowned and busied herself with meal preparations.

"You wouldn't say that if you saw the state Robert Girding was in when we showed him the note and the photo," Parlour replied and proceeded to flick thorough the day's post. "And he has a little girl, too."

"I didn't realise that," Juliet said quietly, stopping in her tracks. *How hideous...*

"I'm sure I told you," Parlour murmured. It wasn't her fault, he knew. He'd been told that it was not uncommon for new mums to become scatty following childbirth. He supposed it was the sudden requirement to consider the needs of another human being, one that couldn't fend for itself, that caused some kind of subconscious filtering process to occur in the brain, rejecting the information that was not directly relevant to either mother or child. Men had been doing the filtering thing for centuries, after all, Parlour thought to himself, usually between the hours of six and eight in the evening. He shouldn't be too hard on Jules.

"So what will you do next?" Juliet asked after a moment.

"We need to have a look round Girding's house again tomorrow, double-check with the neighbours and the locals that no-one saw her. There should be more people around on a Saturday. We've already asked the immediate neighbours and paid a visit to the local convenience store, but I guess we need to widen the net."

"Check his house for what exactly?" Juliet frowned. "You don't suspect Girding of some kind of insurance scam, do you?"

"Personally, no, but I can't rule it out, and I also can't rule out that Lorraine Girding had some kind of secret that may help explain her abduction. Or I may simply find some clue to her whereabouts that the others didn't spot."

"You're going to personally search the house?" Juliet enquired.

"Think I need to," Parlour nodded. "Delegation has its place, but it hasn't done me any favours so far. Sounds arrogant, I know, but I trust my own powers of observation above those of the rest of the crew."

"Even the divine Karen?" Juliet asked sarcastically.

"DI Preece isn't closely involved in this case, Jules," Parlour replied stiffly. "Goodlove's my man on this one."

"Should I be jealous?" Juliet giggled.

Parlour laughed, glad for a lightening of the atmosphere, and glad he had his back to Jules at that precise moment, lest she should see the pained glance that flashed across his cheeks at the mention of Karen Preece's name.

14

Saturday 12 November 2011

"Afternoon, Karen," Parlour remarked dryly as a freshly showered DI Preece entered the incident room at ten past ten the following morning. "Overslept did we? Not like you."

Underslept more like, Preece thought to herself, extremely pleasurable memories of the night before flooding her head once more.

"Sorry boss, caught a film with a mate in Reading last night. Stayed over and missed the early train back."

"Spare me the details, Preece," Parlour said, swatting his hand vaguely in her direction, though the daggers of jealousy were jabbing his innards. Karen Preece did not go in for girly nights out at the flicks, as a rule.

"Funny thing happened though, boss," Preece continued, following Parlour back to his office.

He turned and faced her, hand on the door handle. "Look, Karen, I'm up to my neck in it. If it's nothing to do with the case, then I'm not interested."

Oooh, touchy, Preece thought, dimly aware of a strange pained expression on her DCI's face, but too full of euphoria from the previous evening to give it any further thought.

"It's not. Just think I might have an interesting fraud case for you, that's all."

Parlour sighed and sat down. "I'm sorry, Karen. We have a kidnapping on our hands, but no leads and not an inkling where the woman's being kept. And now it looks like they're planning more abductions. I have the Superintendent ranting and raving at me, and to make it worse, I've had no sleep."

You and me both, Preece thought to herself, trying not to grin, every muscle in her body relaxed from the previous evening's pleasures.

"Spill the beans, then," Parlour said, attempting an interested smile and ending up grimacing at his junior colleague instead.

"Seen *Gorilla Wars* yet?" Preece enquired, leaning over his desk, palms of her hands on its beech veneer.

"You mean that kids' movie that's on at the cinema at the moment?"

"Or is it?" Preece asked enigmatically.

"I'm not in the mood for games, Karen," Parlour said shortly, turning his gaze to his computer monitor and checking his email in vain for leads on the Girding case.

"Went to the cinema last night with this mate of mine. Felt like a bit of light relief, suggested we saw *Gorilla Wars*. It's one of those computer animated jobbies, not Pixar but similar. You must have seen it advertised around Billock - giant poster of a gorilla bursting through some greenery, with a club in his hand."

"It's everywhere in Deverton, too," Parlour conceded. "And the local burger joints are all giving away *Gorilla Wars* toys - the kids at church were all fiddling with them in the service last week. Obviously we wouldn't be seen dead...."

"Obviously not," Preece grinned, cutting short a predictably precious middle-class rant from her superior concerning the evils of fast-food outlets.

"And the relevance of this is?" Parlour asked dryly, eyes darting across his computer screen.

"Have you tried to go and see it?"

Parlour frowned. "Why on earth would I, Karen? Do I look like the kind of intellectual lightweight who goes to watch kids' movies for relaxation?"

"Oh come on, boss, you know what these films are like - half the jokes are aimed at adults. It's not all computer animated bunnies and cheesy moral sound-bites."

Parlour looked up at his newly promoted inspector. "Karen – spare me the film critique; I've neither the time nor the patience this morning for trivialities."

"There's no *Gorilla Wars*!" Preece persevered, clearly pleased with herself. "It's a scam! Billock CineHeaven has never even heard of the film; I called them this morning. They reckon it's some kind of hoax and have ordered that the bill posters be taken down. I've sent a few DCs around the local fast-food joints, to make enquiries about who supplied the toys. Apparently someone's been selling *Gorilla Wars* t-shirts and pencil cases at the local farmers' markets and car-boots, too. Sounds like a half decent scam if you ask me, Sir. Probably made a mint on the merchandising already. Probably even retired on it."

"Probably," Parlour agreed, finally looking up and meeting Preece's dark eyes, an exercise he had been avoiding lately. He leant back in his chair and flexed his hands, stiff from typing frenetically. "Sorry, Karen, I'm snowed under at the moment. Can't you delegate it? Surely it's a matter for the Office of Fair Trading, in the first instance, anyway? I need everyone I can get at the moment. May even need you.."

Preece couldn't deny that her heart skipped a beat at this admission. What was going on with her? Shaun Fox was the smartest, sexiest bit of male kit to come her way in a long time and here she was still lusting after the patronising, pious piece of pock-faced police intelligence that was Mark "Pizza" Parlour.

Karen Preece was still loitering in the doorway when Parlour's phone rang.

"Could you take that, Karen? I was supposed to be at Robert Girding's house with Forensics twenty minutes ago."

"What if they want you, Sir?"

"Just deal with it for me, will you?" Parlour snapped. He grabbed his heavy winter coat off the back of the door and pushed past her en route to the staff car-park, not meeting her eye.

Shaking her head at her boss's demeanour, Karen Preece took the call. It wasn't good news.

15

The call, put through to CID immediately by the Desk Sergeant, was from a Mr Adam Beckford. He had returned home in the early hours of Saturday morning to find his wife missing. As with Lorraine Girding, her vital possessions were still at home, and her car still parked on the driveway. It was, again in common with the Girding case, as if Eve Beckford had been taken away by the fairies. There were no visible signs of a break-in nor a botched burglary, and no indication that Mrs Beckford had ventured outdoors. Both of her choice winter coats were still hanging up in the hallway, and her handbag still lay on the dining room table, complete with keys, mobile phone and credit cards.

Beckford had already checked his wife's phone, diary and kitchen calendar for clues to her whereabouts, fearing he had forgotten some engagement she had reminded him of on countless occasions, as husbands were prone to doing.

Members of the family plus assorted friends and work colleagues had been contacted, but to no avail- it seemed that Eve Beckford, like Lorraine Girding before her, had vanished without trace.

With Goodlove on the hunt for the elusive Lorraine Girding, and Parlour up at Mr Girding's house in Lexington Meadows, Karen Preece was left with no choice but to assume control. Leaving it to DC Jenkins to bring Parlour up to speed on the latest disturbing revelation, Preece nabbed a junior colleague and made the short drive across town to the Beckford's home on the eastern outskirts of Billock.

Within ten minutes, she was ringing on the doorbell of the Beckford residence.

"Detective Inspector Karen Preece, Billock CID. We just talked on the phone. And this is Detective Constable Leanne Quinn."

"Which one's Cagney?" Beckford quipped nervously, standing aside to admit the two women into his hallway.

"We're more Jordan and McIntyre, if you're up on your Val McDermid," Karen stated drily, as Beckford shut the door behind them. She noted that he had done a quick recky to see if anyone had seen them enter. He was clearly a man who cared what the neighbours thought.

"I'm not, but come through anyway." Beckford led them into a spacious pale blue living room, the walls covered with expansive canvas shots of, presumably, his wife and kids. They were the sort of staged family photos that cost a small fortune and featured families lolling unnaturally on white dust-sheets in allegedly relaxed poses. There was something curiously passionless about the photos, Preece thought, as if they'd been taken for the sake of it, as a decorative feature, rather than a symbol of family unity.

"Sorry to get you out of bed on a Saturday," Beckford apologised.

"Most of the CID team are working today, anyway," Preece replied, declining to mention precisely why. There was no sense in terrifying the man before they had any hard evidence that the two disappearances were linked.

"Your wife and children, I take it?" Quinn indicated towards the largest canvas print above the fireplace.

"Yes, that's Eve and the girls. Mindy's six and Perdita's three and a half."

Preece gave Quinn a hard stare, hoping she would not enquire where Pongo was, or make any other further allusions to the remaining 101 Dalmatians.

"Where are the girls, Sir?" DC Quinn enquired.

"They're still at their grandmother's. They attend Saint Anna's Prep School. They had half-term this week. Eve was going to collect them today."

"Bit late, isn't it?" Quinn frowned, whose niece and nephew had definitely been at school the past few weeks.

"Saint Anna's has its own terms," Beckford replied. Was it Preece's imagination, or did Beckford sound a mite embarrassed at their choice of school?

"Eve was taking the week off work to decorate upstairs, then she was going to collect the girls from her mother's this morning. She wanted us all out of the way, to have a clear run at it – the decorating, I mean. It made sense to do it this week, with the girls away and me in Germany."

"Where does your mother-in-law live, then?" Preece asked.

"Just past Ringwood. Not so far."

"But she obviously hadn't gone early? That's her car in the driveway, right?"

Beckford confirmed that the silver Volvo outside was indeed his wife's.

"And you've been away on a business trip, I understand?" Preece enquired, checking her notepad.

Beckford nodded. "I've been in Frankfurt since Tuesday, at a pharmaceutical conference."

"And when was the last time you spoke to your wife?"

Beckford looked sheepish. "I never ring when I'm away."

Preece looked up sharply. "Oh?"

"I sent a text to say I'd arrived safely on Tuesday, that's all Eve likes me to do. Eve's not the clingy type. She just wanted to get on."

Preece shot Quinn a sidelong glance that spelt *odd*. "What about your mother-in-law? Your wife must have rung there, to speak to the girls?"

Beckford shook his head. Miranda Faulkner, Eve's mother, had been contacted, but hadn't talked to her daughter since Eve had dropped the children off on Tuesday morning.

"Surely your wife would at least ring the girls?" Preece frowned. Beckford looked embarrassed again and averted his gaze from the straight-talking DI. "Eve's funny like that. She likes to compartmentalise people, emotions, situations... ife girls are at their grandmother's, then they're being cared for and they're OK. They don't need a phone call, from Eve's perspective. She's very self-sufficient... I guess, she just expects everyone else to feel the same way. She gets it from her mother. Miranda calls on a needs-must basis, too."

Poor sod, Preece thought to herself, sensing the wistful tone in Beckford's voice. Here was a man who had fallen hopelessly in love with an ice maiden and hoped to melt her heart through time. But snow leopards rarely changed their spots, in Preece's experience.

He had it all in material terms; the beautiful wife, the trophy daughters, the fantastic house. But in real terms, he was an empty shell of a man. She wouldn't blame him one iota if he sought solace in a stranger's arms... and perhaps that was exactly what he did on those interminable conferences of his. That is, if there had been a conference in the first place.

"So ostensibly, Eve could have disappeared anytime from Tuesday onwards? You've had no contact from her? Or did she reply to your initial text at least?"

"She texted *OK, have a good week*, or something of that ilk, on Tuesday lunchtime, about one o'clock. Other than that, we've not spoken."

Preece made a note to check their phones. As stated in their earlier telephone conversation, there were no obvious signs as to the whereabouts of Mrs Beckford, and no indications whatsoever that she had left the house. Beckford said that he had rung all those acquaintances of Eve's known to him, but to no avail. Nobody had a clue where she could have got to, and she had made no contact with any friends or family from Tuesday onwards.

"Before I circulate her details, I need to send a team over to have a look around the house, if that's alright with you?" Preece checked. She was sure Parlour wouldn't want her to inform Beckford of Lorraine Girding's disappearance at this delicate juncture.

Beckford frowned. "Why? I haven't locked her under the stairs, or buried her beneath the patio, if that's what you're thinking!"

Preece glanced at Quinn. Who had mentioned murder? Was it significant? Beckford did seem more than a little edgy. Preece decided to give him the benefit of the doubt at this juncture.

"It's just routine," she lied. Assuming Beckford was entirely innocent, it would not do to scare him half to death at this point by suggesting his wife had been abducted by some serious creeps that would stop at nothing to earn a fast buck. Details of Lorraine Girding's abduction had not been released to the public as yet. It couldn't be taken for granted that the two disappearances were linked, however likely it appeared. All the same, it was prudent to assume that they were, and to act accordingly. Presumably Beckford would have mentioned a ransom note, had he received one. Preece was not about to put the proverbial willies up him by posing the question.

"We need to look for signs of illegal entry, that kind of thing," she smiled matter-of-factly at Beckford.

"Where do you work, Sir?" DC Quinn enquired, all too aware that Girding had received a ransom note anonymously through his office door.

"I'm MD of a pharmaceutical company in Foxburgh," Beckford replied. "Wessex Medicare, we're based at Coving Industrial Park."

Quinn nodded, taking notes. She looked up. "And your wife?"

"Eve has a little part-time number at a fashion boutique in Billock. They do evening wear, dress-hire, you know the like."

"Ten til two or something?" Preece asked.

"Yeah, term times only. It's a pretty flexible arrangement. Jenni, that's the owner of the boutique, is a long-standing friend of Eve's."

"And the name of the boutique?"

"*All that Jazz*," Beckford smiled, in spite of the circumstances. "You know, from *Chicago.*"

Preece looked blank. She was not a fan of musicals.

The smile disappeared from Beckford's face as he considered his beautiful wife's portrait on the wall.

"She's a very attractive woman," Preece agreed, contemplating the tanned, rather equine lady with wavy blonde hair and a somewhat distant expression. Her eyes were an alarming shade of turquoise. Tinted contact lenses, perhaps? Vanity drove the modern woman to quite bizarre extremes, Karen thought. She was not one for cosmetic enhancements; a decision made easier by nature's own benevolence towards her – with the possible exception of the bosom department. She jotted down a few further notes then snapped her notebook shut.

"The Police Family Liaison Officer will be here in a minute, and I expect you'll receive a visit soon from my senior colleague, DCI Parlour, too. I'm … erm… on another case at the moment and I expect he'll take over from me."

"Whatever," Beckford shrugged, not realising the significance of Preece handing over the reins to a more senior officer. "I just want Eve back safe and sound."

"We'll do our very best," Preece said tightly.

16

Parlour didn't know whether to be more upset about the further twist in the case, or at Preece handling the interview with Adam Beckford. In the end, he had taken a well-advised two minutes out to kick the gable wall of Robert Girding's five bed detached, before arranging a team meeting back at base. His presence at Girding's house that morning had more to do with the need to feel busy than an actual requirement to be there. As Senior Investigating Officer, Parlour's job was to oversee operations and handle the media, but the Control Freak in him had never been good at standing back from the action, and it was too soon to issue a press release on the missing woman at this point. But now that news had come through of a second abduction, Parlour would have to leave the crime team to it at Girding's house. Forensics could call him with any new findings; for now he needed to get up to speed with the latest events and formulate a plan of action on the assumption that Beckford would soon be on the receiving end of a ransom note, too.

Preece had already paid a visit to Wessex Medicare on the Coving Industrial Park and had managed to gain access to Adam Beckford's unopened mail by flashing a badge and a winning smile at the nervous young man on reception. Some middle-aged men in weekend casuals were in the building, clearly putting in some overtime in a valiant attempt to boost sales figures. Either that, or they were avoiding the rigours of shared childcare, Preece had thought cynically to herself. There were no demands for money among the copious sales analyses and sales figures on Beckford's desk.

By the time all the available members of Billock CID were assembled in the Incident Room just before noon, Parlour had projected several digital images of the missing women on the wall. Alongside the smiling picture of Lorraine Girding was the rather grainy image of a bound and gagged Mrs Girding, sent to Robert Girding's office by her abductors.

"Good morning everyone," Parlour began soberly. "I understand DS Goodlove has briefed you all on the background of Mrs Lorraine Girding and the events surrounding her disappearance."

There was a murmur of confirmation.

"Good. There's more bad news, I'm afraid. We've received news of another missing woman this morning, and though we don't know for sure that the two cases are linked, we need to assume for the moment that they are. The second missing woman is a Mrs Eve Beckford, aged thirty-five. She went missing sometime between Tuesday lunchtime and around 3 am this morning, when her husband returned from a business trip. She's mother to two little girls aged six and three. She works part-time in a fashion boutique in Billock. Her husband, would you *Adam and Eve it*, is actually called Adam, and is MD of Wessex Medicare in Foxburgh on the Coving Estate. They live in a smart detached house in Eastlands Phase Two, here in Billock."

"I barely need to point out the similarities, but will anyway:- both women are attractive, well-turned out mothers and wives of successful husbands - a species I believe are colloquially known as Yummy Mummies. Both women are car-drivers and have a small income of their own. Both live in attractive detached properties in well-heeled areas. Neither woman appeared to have left the house, as in both cases, their cars and vital possessions were found at the property. In both cases, too, nobody has any idea where they could have got to. We're double checking with the neighbours and local area in the case of Lorraine Girding, but so far, nobody spotted her on the afternoon or evening of Wednesday 9 November."

"We haven't got that far in the case of Eve Beckford, but we're onto it. There's no sign of a ransom note so far in the Beckford case, but it's early days."

Parlour paused for breath.

"As you know, Girding was instructed to leave £50k in notes in a cereal box in Fryer's Dip - the heath-land behind Billock Towers high-rise. This was duly done, but the kidnappers probably got wind of the undercover police surveillance operation and acted accordingly. The money was grabbed by a hoodie on two wheels, who was unfortunately allowed to escape by the undercover unit. Robert Girding was then sent a note telling him that he should have obeyed instructions and not involved the police, along with a printed image of a gagged and bound Lorraine Girding. This note intimated that the kidnappers were planning a further abduction."

"The good news is, Forensics are sure it's Lorraine Girding and that she's alive in the photo; the bad news is, she could already be dead of course. If she isn't, her abductors have threatened to kill her if we intervene in the next ransom handover."

Parlour used his infra-red pointer to indicate to the second communication from the kidnappers, copied onto a PowerPoint slide.

"Before we move onto Mrs Beckford, are Forensics convinced beyond a shadow of a doubt that the woman in the photo is Lorraine Girding?" DC Quinn enquired.

"Unless they have a Lorraine Girding lookalike and an Oscar-nominated make-up artist on spot in their secret hideaway, there's every indication from the photographic evidence that this is our woman."

Parlour surveyed his team.

"At this point, we're waiting for a ransom note before we officially link the two disappearances and inform both parties concerned. Meanwhile, we proceed with door to door enquiries in both Lexington and the Eastlands Estate to try and find some clue to the ladies' whereabouts."

"And do we know which woman was abducted first?" Preece enquired.

"Presumably Lorraine Girding because the ransom note has come through already, but not necessarily," Parlour replied.

"And would you say there's a financial motive at work here, rather than a sexual one?" Preece continued, who had been drafted onto the case now that a second woman had been abducted.

"Difficult to say for sure until the next ransom note appears," Parlour replied. "But given the relatively secure financial status of both women in question, I'd say it was more likely the kidnappers see the husbands as cash cows. However, that's not to rule out some kind of link between the two women beyond the obviously financial motive. So I need you to get cracking on any possible links between the two women, Karen."

Parlour stared pointedly at her and she flushed slightly, nodding. Parlour was interrupted at this point by a junior officer, who handed him a print out of an email from Forensics.

He frowned, perusing its contents. "This is from Forensics over at Robert Girding's house. Imprints in the gravel driveway suggest a van of some description pulled up at the door on the day of her disappearance. They've also found a kitchen calendar stuck inside one of the cupboards that Girding did not seem to be aware of. The letter "B" is written on the day in question, circled in biro. Can't think off the top of my head what that could be. But can someone check out any friends or relatives with names beginning with that letter, or perhaps clubs or organisations that Mrs Girding was affiliated to. I don't think for one minute she met up with her cronies at the local Castle Bingo, though," Parlour added dryly.

"Perhaps she scheduled in a weekly bonk on a Wednesday afternoon?" DC Denton grinned. "Or perhaps she was into a bit of bond…"

Parlour held his hand up. "That's enough. I'll be in my office if any of you want me, otherwise DS Goodlove will give you all your jobs."

Karen Preece did want Parlour; she also needed to have a word about the Girding/Beckford abductions. Ignoring the puppy dog noises emanating from Sean Denton's desk, she followed Parlour across the room, wincing as she whacked her upper thigh on a desk corner in her haste to catch up with her senior colleague.

"Karen..." Parlour stated listlessly, who had sincerely hoped no-one would take him up on his empty offer to further discuss the case.

"Boss, there's something bothering me," Preece frowned, wishing Parlour would meet her gaze instead of fiddling with his desktop computer the whole time.

"Well, there's some*one* bothering me, and if I don't start making headway with this case, the proverbial poo is going to hit the fan," Parlour replied stressily.

"Must be hard, Sir," Karen replied, trying to introduce a lighter note to the exchange. "Being knee-deep in the stuff at home and in the workplace!"

Parlour just looked at her. "What is it, Karen? I don't have time to discuss FakeFlixGate, if that's what you've..."

"No Sir, I've handed that one over to Jenkins. It's about the missing women."

"Well? Spit it out!"

"Do you not think, Sir," Preece began tentatively, "that we should be looking a little more closely at Robert Girding and Adam Beckford themselves, and not just the wives?"

"We've done preliminary background checks on both men, Karen," Parlour replied impatiently. "They're both clean as a whistle, no skeletons in the closet, no reason to suspect they're anything other than helpless victims of an organised gang after some serious lolly."

"I mean, whether they're in any way linked personally," Preece persisted.

Parlour frowned. "Of course they're linked; both have wives who've been abducted in similarly mysterious circumstances."

"I don't mean that, Sir," Karen looked perplexed. Was he being deliberately dim?

"Karen!" Parlour exclaimed, fingers to his temples. She saw the colour rising up his pale neck; a bodily reaction it was hard for one with Parlour's colouring to disguise.

"We have DCs and uniform looking closely into the lives of the Girdings *and* the Beckfords, I can assure you," Parlour stated coldly, meeting her briefly in the eye.

"With respect, Sir, they don't appear to be coming up with much," Preece stated resolutely, jutting her chin out.

"*With respect*, DI Preece," Parlour retorted acerbically, "You've been out the office a lot catching the latest flix, so you're maybe not up to speed yourself."

"Ouch," Preece stated dryly and shook her head at Parlour.

Her senior colleague was clearly rattled, and Preece was sufficiently self-aware to know that it wasn't just the pressures of the case or difficulties at home.

17

Monday 14 November 2011

Parlour tossed and turned all night, mobile phone next to his radio alarm, lest he miss an important progression in the case. The remainder of the weekend had been spent frenetically interviewing neighbours in the vicinity of Girding and Beckford's homes in Lexington and Billock respectively. Unfortunately, as was often the case in affluent neighbourhoods such as these, all manner of vans and trade vehicles passed by and pulled up at various houses at all hours of the day. These were not people averse to paying money for goods and services; Eve Beckford's decision to decorate her own upstairs was one borne of personal choice rather than financial necessity, being one of those breed of women, usually affluent and middle-class, who enjoyed stencilling and scrap-booking and other rather trivial pursuits of a purely cosmetic nature.

Nobody had spotted anybody or anything out of the ordinary. No suspicious persons or vehicular activity had been reported in the vicinity of either house. And so there was nothing to be done but wait until the morning, in the hope that one of his team had turned up some vital piece of information. Hopefully that would be the only overnight development.

Unable to get to sleep and feeling the beginnings of a head-cold coming on, Parlour got up and made himself a Whisky-Lemsip cocktail. That usually helped him nod off. The concoction did the trick and within fifteen minutes, Parlour was swirling around subconsciously in a bizarre chemically enhanced underworld of misplaced affections and inappropriate actions. It was with his tongue eagerly exploring the neck of a leather-clad Karen Preece that he was brought up to the surface by his radio alarm at 7.00 am.

He patted the duvet absent-mindedly but the familiar bulk of his wife's increasingly voluptuous body was absent. Grabbing his dressing gown, Parlour wandered downstairs, where he found Juliet dozily giving Rowan a bottle in front of the BBC Breakfast News headlines.

"Ro slept through!" Parlour noted, yawning and stretching his arms out sideways.

"Pardon?"

"I said, Ro slept through! That's brilliant!"

"Can't quite believe it, actually," Juliet conceded. "Must let him nap all afternoon more often!"

"Do you think he's coming down with something, though?" Parlour wondered, feeling his baby son's soft, warm forehead. Rowan raised his blue eyes to his father's matching set briefly before staring back down at the bottle in his mouth. "I mean, it's very abnormal for him to sleep so much."

"Cynic!" Juliet laughed. It was good to hear her laugh again. She seemed a lot more chirpy, Parlour thought.

"All the same, I wouldn't let him nap all afternoon again," Parlour stated.

"I'll take him out for some fresh air after lunch," Juliet replied. "I was thinking of driving to Foxburgh and doing a little window shopping. Ought to start thinking about Christmas soon."

Parlour groaned.

"Now who's the cynic?" Juliet grinned. "Come on, Mark, it's our first Christmas with a baby - it'll be lovely this year!"

"I don't suppose there's any chance we can just spend it alone?" Parlour wondered aloud in a defeated tone of voice.

Juliet just looked at him reproachfully and squeezed the air out of the teat of the bottle. While she conceded that spontaneity was a swear word to her parents, who sucked the life out of Christmas with their desire to control every second of the festive season, they were still her parents after all. At least they lived locally and actually wanted to see the family, unlike Richard and Anne Parlour, who had bought themselves a hideaway cottage on the Cornish coast as a retirement present to themselves. Unfortunately for Parlour, who regretted the increasing emotional distance between his parents and himself, the transfer to the West Country signified not only a retirement from their professional lives, but a retirement from society *per se*. It was also a very clear statement on the importance that family life held to the Senior Parlours – namely, *zilch*. This unwritten message cut right through Parlour's cop-hardened exterior.

Neither Parlour nor his younger brother had enjoyed a particularly close bond with his parents. Richard Parlour had worked for the Security Services and whilst that had fuelled in Parlour an early interest in security and police related matters, it had simultaneously created a certain distance between his father and himself. Parlour Senior was unable to discuss his work with either of his sons, and with restrictions placed on phone-calls and visits to the family home, both boys had grown up in a rather secretive, isolated environment. Anne Parlour, however, a full-time housewife, had dedicated herself to the welfare of her sons, and her steady, loving hand had ensured that both boys grew up to be well-balanced individuals, if a little too distant and self-contained as a result of the discretion that had to be exercised at all times due to Parlour Senior's position.

It seemed that the reclusive lifestyle was rather too ingrained by now for the elder Parlours to contemplate a life which integrated either son. Whilst Mark and Juliet had no desire for either set of parents to camp on their doorstep, a little more involvement and interest in their day to day life from Mark's parents would have been welcome, especially in these difficult months of adjusting to parenthood.

Parlour could not help but feel a little pang of jealousy every time he walked past a play-park and saw doting grandparents pushing toddlers on swings. He could not imagine either of his parents performing an activity that was commonplace for so many people of their age and status – maybe his mother at an absolute push, but only if she escaped the tyranny of her domineering and reclusive husband for long enough to make the five hour trip to Hampshire. It was a big "if" and not one Parlour saw being realised in their lifetime.

For all their petty rules and regulations and neo-Thatcherist tendencies, Parlour had to pay grudging respect to Juliet's parents, Derek and Margaret Hebble. At least they tried, in their own awkward and fastidious way, to be involved in the life of their daughter and grandson. It did not come naturally, and there were precious few concessions to the modern way of rearing children, which encouraged independence and freedom of expression, even at a very early age. Though both Hebbles faced a constant battle to suppress their inner Victorian, they were gradually learning to love little Rowan, with his noisy yelps and sicky burps.

With this mounting affection for their only grandson came increasing offers of help, for which Juliet and Mark were very grateful. Nevertheless, Juliet was still glad they had made the move to the new town of Deverton. True, their house in Billock had boasted considerably more character than their red-brick new build in Spatchcock Drive. It also had to be (grudgingly) acknowledged that the town centre of Billock offered far more in the way of local amenities than the still rather limited Deverton. Yet, all things considered, it remained preferable to be a safe distance from the parental home and Juliet did not regret their decision to relocate.

A good twenty minute drive away from Billock, and with no out of town retail outlets or other such attractions to lure the Hebbles westwards, Deverton was the perfect location for the Parlours. It enabled Parlour to commute easily to Billock Police HQ without fearing acts of reprisal on his property, an unpleasant side-effect of his time in Billock. Parlour's vulnerable position as a high-ranking police officer living locally had been exacerbated by his impressive track-record of putting murderers and other serious criminals behind bars.

Life had been rather more sedate of late, though. Whilst Parlour had no shortage of work to plough through, there had been no high profile cases to get the old juices flowing. Until now.

The chilling ransom note arrived by first class post to Wessex Medicare later that morning. Like its predecessor, it requested that Adam Beckford left £50k in waterproof packaging inside a Value cereal box at 20.00 hrs that evening, again next to the electricity substation in Fryer's Dip. Any police involvement, and "both women" in their possession would be killed. At least they'd stopped at two... so far.

The only anomaly was that this time the outer packaging was to be a Value Wheat Biscuits box.

18

"It's absolutely brilliant, Parlour," Superintendent Dewhurst stated, shaking his head in admiration across the conference room table just after noon. "You have to admit it – not your traditional Pay And She Goes tactic. Beckford doesn't just have the skin of his own wife to save, but Robert Girding's missus as well. The pressure on him to cough up £50k is intolerable."

"There's no issue of him not drawing out the dough, Sir," Parlour said quietly, who did not share his senior officer's ability to detach himself sufficiently from the crime to marvel at its ingenuity. "It's getting a march on the kidnappers somehow without being seen to be involved at the handover."

"What are your plans, then?" Superintendent Chris Dewhurst inquired. With this surname, it was unsurprising that he was known by all and sundry as The Sausage. Indeed, with his shiny pate and jowly pink features, he was not unlike a large pink lump of sausage-meat, stuffed into the external skin of an M&S suit gasping at the seams. By comparison, Parlour was a mere chipolata of a man, barely filling the seat of his pants.

"I won't draft in a surveillance unit," Parlour stated.

"Probably best after the last spectacular cock-up," Dewhurst agreed.

Parlour ignored him.

I thought this was supposed to be a brain-storming session, Parlour thought disconsolately, sensing Dewhurst was simply seizing another opportunity to bring Parlour down a peg or two rather than offer up any helpful suggestions as to how they might best catch the abductors.

"I'm not sure we should even try and rig up some cameras in the trees. However far in advance we do it, they might spot them and who knows what they'll do to our women. We're probably being watched through a pair of binoculars by a resident of the high-rise – or just as likely, a visitor to one of the residents."

"So what alternatives are there?" Dewhurst asked impatiently, drumming his porky fingers on the table.

"Do nothing. Beckford places the money there, comes home, hopefully the women are released." Parlour's facial expression suggested he did not consider this a viable option.

"And what's wrong with that plan, other than Beckford being down £50k?" Dewhurst enquired.

"We gain no lead on the identity or whereabouts of the kidnappers."

"And does that matter if the women are released?"

"They may not release them, and in any case, the kidnappers could strike again," Parlour replied perfunctorily.

"Mrs Girding and Mrs Beckford may be able to give us some clues," Dewhurst stated.

"Which is why they may not release them or may harm them."

"What do you think they'll do?"

Parlour weighed up the question. "Depends how much dosh they're after. It's far more difficult to keep two women in captivity than just the one. We don't know how depraved these people are. If it were me, I'd release them somewhere in the back of beyond to give me time to make a getaway. But we can't rule out the fact that they may well renege on their word and kill the women anyway, to stop them blabbing. Obviously, though, they've then got a double murder charge hanging over them if they get caught, which may act as a deterrent. It's all a bit of a lottery when you're dealing with callous monsters like this."

"You know what I don't get, Parlour," Dewhurst stated, rather transparently playing at Devil's Advocate once more in an attempt to get Parlour's cogs working more smoothly. In the Superintendent's view, parenthood was beginning to addle his DCI's brains. Parlour was not the sharpest Sabatier in the knife-block at the moment, it had to be said.

"What's that, Sir?" Parlour replied wearily, fed up of the puerile and unsubtle tactics of his senior colleague.

"Why bother with such middle-class small fry, for £50k apiece? I mean, why not go for it and nab the wife of some multimillionaire society toff? Why not three million smackers in a briefcase; what's with the loose change in a cheapo cereal box?"

Wish I had £50k in loose change, Parlour thought to himself. Something suddenly struck him as being relevant in Dewhurst's comment, but the thought flew out of his head as rapidly as it flew in.

"I guess it's an issue of accessibility," Parlour replied. "Rich women don't open doors to tradesmen; they have housekeepers or personal assistants. And they tend to be conspicuous whilst out and about; they're not anonymous members of society that you could whisk off down a side-street."

"So how do our kidnappers know the financial status of our two women, given that they're not exactly in the public eye? It's not as if they're listed in *Who's Who* or anything. Have you considered a personal link between the two?"

"Of course I have," Parlour replied impatiently, insulted that Dewhurst should even suggest he would ignore such an obvious line of enquiry. "The two women did not know each other, as far as we know and ditto the husbands."

"What about indirect links between the two women?"

"They don't share a bank or building society; we've no reason to suspect any bank employees of involvement in the kidnappings. I can see no link between the women, other than their shared status as wives of well-paid, successful professional men."

"Perhaps they both use the same mail order catalogue or something of that ilk? We're looking for insider knowledge of their financial status."

"Leanne Quinn is looking into it, Sir," Parlour replied dutifully, feeling thoroughly patronised.

"So how are we going to catch the kidnappers?" Dewhurst wondered aloud, drumming even more audibly on the table.

"Well, the tracking devices failed miserably first time round – but I expect we'll persevere with them," Parlour replied.

"Isn't there a risk they'll spot them and your women are "dead meat" all the same?"

"You've seen the size of them these days - smaller than a shirt button, Sir," Parlour replied.

"Well you better get onto it pronto, then, if Beckford's going to get those notes sorted for 8pm."

"I've already got Technical Support onto it," Parlour stated.

"And you say the trackers failed first time round?" Dewhurst checked.

"They don't communicate through water, do they, Sir? We think the kidnappers asked for the money to be placed in a waterproof bag because they were going to submerse it in water."

"We're not dealing with novices, then?" Dewhurst frowned.

"It would seem not, Sir, though it's surprising how much you can pick up from TV crime dramas."

"Shame your team didn't pick up enough information on how to keep hold of a suspect, Parlour," Dewhurst remarked dryly.

"We thought we had the place sufficiently staked out," Parlour said gloomily. "I didn't bank on Rushton and Mitchell letting me down."

"I hope they got a right bollocking," Dewhurst exclaimed. "I'd have stuck them on school visits for the rest of the year."

"They've been disciplined, Sir," Parlour responded wearily, frustrated as ever by Dewhurst's tendency to focus on the negative. "It's not good for morale to harp on about our failures indefinitely."

"All very well, Parlour, but..."

"What are *your* thoughts on the case, Sir?" Parlour interrupted him pointedly.

Dewhurst shuffled his papers and stood up laboriously. "My thoughts are, you'd better not balls-up, Parlour."

Constructive to the last, Parlour thought to himself, following in his considerable wake.

***

Fudge-cakes, Juliet Parlour ersatz-swore to herself, inspecting the contents of her carousel cupboard. In her excitement at the huge range of baby food flavours to choose from at BestCo last week, it had entirely slipped her mind to stock up on Baby Milk.

There's nothing left in Mum's Dairy, Juliet thought wistfully, staring at the rather shapeless lumpy bags that used to be her pert, if rather buxom, breasts. She swivelled the carousel round one more time inside her large store cupboard, but it was no use. She had clean forgotten to buy baby formula. Juliet sighed, staring down at Rowan, who was sucking his thumb peaceably in his baby-bouncer. He looked as if low-fat spread wouldn't liquify in his cute hamster cheeks. She really couldn't face another trek to the supermarket; they only sold the cheapest variety at an inflated price in the local one-stop, which had a constipatory effect on Rowan. But she would have to do something; by her calculations, the current supply would run out by the mid-afternoon feed tomorrow.

Suddenly Juliet had a brainwave. She fetched her laptop and brought up the BestCo homepage. Maybe, just maybe, she could bring forward her delivery slot and get the formula delivered tomorrow along with the rest of the weekly shop. She logged in and clicked on the on-line groceries tab.

Recent orders, current order... change delivery slot! Juliet punched the button enthusiastically and scrolled down a list of

91

dates. *Would you Adam and Eve it*, she exclaimed out loud, the irony of the expression in the current circumstances lost on her.

There was actually an available slot tomorrow lunchtime, from noon till 2pm. They must have had a cancellation, Juliet thought to herself, as every other slot surrounding it was scored out in blue. What a shower from Heaven, Juliet grinned, who didn't believe in luck. Fancy the only free slot this week falling just before Rowan's milk would run out. Juliet was far too much of a novice to the whole home delivery experience to consider that they may substitute the baby milk with another brand, or even worse, an entirely unrelated product, such as chocolate milk-shake or moisturising body milk.

Full of Christian cheer and more than a little smattering of smugness, Juliet changed her delivery to tomorrow's date, and logged off the BestCo website.

19

With several miniscule tracking devices attached to the fifty-pound notes inside, Adam Beckford left the Value Wheat Biscuits box in the spot requested at precisely 8pm that evening. He then returned to his black BMW 4x4 and drove home to await news of his wife.

There was no news.

Back at Billock Police Station, Mark Parlour and two Technical Support Officers swore as the signal went dead on the tracking devices.

"Do you think they're wise to them?" Parlour asked nervously. The lives of two women were on his head. Sergeant Michael Deacon nodded. "Reckon they've almost certainly submersed the bag of cash in a bucket of water. We know that would break communication and it *would* explain why they insisted on the cash being placed in a waterproof bag. It's not just to ward off the elements. "

Parlour smacked the table hard and kicked a metal bin in the corner, which made an almighty din. It did little to appease him.

"What do you want us to do, Sir?" Constable Paul Brodie enquired after an awkward moment.

"There's nothing we can do but sit and wait, is there?" Parlour groaned.

"They'll have to remove the notes from the bag at some point, Sir," Brodie stated hopefully.

"I suspect they will remove the devices almost immediately, since they appear to know what they're doing," Parlour replied gloomily.

"We can at least find out where the money is paid in, assuming they do so straight away," Brodie persevered.

"They're hardly going to pay it in at the local Barclays, are they?"

Parlour scoffed. "Or at any Barclays for that matter. We've put all the financial institutions on red alert for the notes in question, as we did first time round. They'll launder it somehow. We can't have every single business in the country on alert for the banknotes, and certainly not by tomorrow morning – they'll get rid of the stash asap, I would have thought. Probably change it into Euros over the channel or something."

"So what are you going to do?" Brodie enquired.

"I can't just hang around here trashing the office," Parlour groaned. "I'm getting more men out on the streets near Fryer's Dip. Someone must have seen someone speed away on a bike, or acting suspiciously in the area. Think I'll join them."

"Won't your missus need you?" Deacon asked, whose wife had given birth to a baby girl around the same time as Juliet. "It's pretty late; you'll be the first to know if we turn up anything. We all know The Sausage is on your back."

"Jules will be fine," Parlour said less than convincingly. "I'm not much good at this delegation lark. I'd rather be on the front-line. At least I'll only have myself to blame if things go wrong."

What sort of fighting talk was that? Parlour thought to himself, as he made his way back to the Incident Room. He knew he wasn't on good form at the moment; his lack of drive and enthusiasm was beginning to worry him. Maybe the increasingly deskbound nature of his job was beginning to dull his senses. They say you lost muscle tone if you sat around too much; perhaps your brain turned to mush as well.

"Are you alright, boss?" Karen Preece enquired, as Parlour approached her desk. She put the telephone handset down after another line of enquiry died in the water.

"What do you think?" Parlour growled, scanning the update board for the slightest glimmer of success in any of their attempts to track down the missing women. He turned and faced his junior colleague. "I'm heading out to Fryer's Dip.

Can't sit around here doing nothing. Are you here on your lonesome?"

"That new Office Manager is around somewhere, so I'm not chained to the desk - it just looks like it. Want some company?"

"Thought you had a million and one phone calls to make," Parlour stated, alluding to an earlier conversation in CID. Preece had bitten Denton's head off for suggesting she abandoned her post and played teasmaid to them all. It had been a misguided attempt at lightening the atmosphere.

"I've eliminated every possible line of enquiry I can think of. I've found no link between the two families in question, not even a vague acquaintance in common. And I still have no idea what the "B" on Lorraine Girding's kitchen calendar stands for."

"There's no "B" on Eve Beckford's calendar, then, I take it?" Parlour double-checked.

Preece shook her head. "There's no clue in their diaries or on their mobile phones, either."

"Did either of them use a Blackberry or an iPhone?"

"Nope.   Not high-powered enough... or pretentious enough," commented Preece, who was not into gadgets for gadget's sake, unlike Parlour, who liked nothing better than to pore over the instructions of a pointless piece of electronic kit on Christmas Day.

Unless one was employed by the Security or Emergency Services, Karen Preece could see no logical reason why ordinary citizens living largely humdrum existences should feel the need to be contactable at all times. Affordable mobile communications technology had given individuals a disproportionate sense of self-importance which bordered on the farcical, as far as Preece was concerned. So occupied were these people in communicating the minutiae of their own lives to others, via texts and tweets and social networking sites, very little valuable human productivity actually took place. Far from being in the thick of the action, these angst-ridden individuals were swept up in a sea of inertia. Or, at least that was Karen Preece's take on modern society.

"And I assume there were no messages on the landline answer phones at either house?"

"Nothing," Preece replied.

"I don't suppose the B on Mrs Girding's calendar could have stood for Beckford? She could have been having an illicit liaison with Adam Beckford..."

"What a nasty, suspicious little mind you have!" Preece grinned.

Parlour shrugged. "Comes with the territory."

"Seems entirely out of character, from what we've learnt of both women – both families – so far. And it's hard to imagine how Lorraine Girding would have come to know Adam Beckford. They might have similar amounts stashed away in the bank, but there endeth the comparison. She's pure class; he's pure chav."

Preece paused. "But I guess it's worth checking out," she conceded. She stood up and stretched her torso upwards to pull a fleece jersey over her head. Parlour felt a twitching in his left front pocket area; he could not help but stare at her small but pert breasts strain against the thin white cotton of her long-sleeved top. He put his hands in his pockets immediately and turned away, feeling an unwelcome flush rise up his pale neck. Cursing under his breath, Parlour returned to his office to grab his coat and car-keys. What sort of Class A idiot was he, suggesting he spend a couple of hours alone with his DI, cruising around Fryer's Dip in the dark?

Parlour was silent as they made the short journey across Billock to the wasteland where the ransom package had been left and subsequently lifted by the abductors. He elected to drive, leaving Preece to deal with incoming calls on the mobile and exchange what precious little police intelligence they had regarding the double kidnapping.

You couldn't get more opposite to Jules if you tried, Parlour thought to himself, considering Karen Preece's profile out of the corner of his eye as he parked up in a lay-by near the quarry. While Juliet was short and curvaceous, Karen was tall and boyish in physique. Juliet was blonde with an expressive, open visage; Karen was raven-haired with deep set eyes which created an air of wary distance between her and the person attempting to connect with her. And, thought Parlour rather uncharitably, Juliet was chubby and out of shape, where Karen was athletic without an ounce of surplus fat on her sinewy limbs. But Karen was not the mother of a much longed-for child. Karen was also not his wife... Juliet was, and there the interior monologue should stop, Parlour told himself firmly.

Unknown to him, Preece was making similarly uncomplimentary physical comparisons between Parlour and Shaun Fox, as she awaited a call-back from DS Goodlove. Fox had barely been in touch since the passionate night they'd spent together. Preece tried not to let it get her down; she knew Fox was under pressure to produce the goods over in Thames Valley, as she was in Hampshire, and felt sure the sexy DI would be in touch again soon.

She was not one to chase after men; whilst she would never "treat em mean and keep em keen", as the old adage went, she wasn't going to make a fool of herself by appearing too enthusiastic. In any case, it might perhaps be prudent to find out a little more about Shaun Fox before she got into any kind of relationship with him. The evening she had spent with him had been extremely pleasurable, with his physical prowess more than complimenting his intellectual powers. Yet she had still left his flat with the uncomfortable feeling that she knew very little about him. Even his apartment had been strangely devoid of information relating to his personal life. The usual ubiquitous Best of CDs had filled a small media cabinet alongside a dozen or so male movie classics. The coffee table had contained the latest edition of GQ; the bookshelves had boasted a few dog-eared Peter Robinsons (Banks Series) and a copy of the Oxford Dictionary. But where were the family photos, the mug-shots of mates pulling stupid stunts stuck to the fridge door? What about the usual paraphernalia found in any lived-in property? Perhaps he was just fastidiously neat and tidy and preferred the minimalist look. Or perhaps he had something to hide? Perhaps he was cruel to small animals and had been violently abused as a child... *Stop it!* Karen berated herself. *You've been working with psychos too long.* She decided to concentrate on his good points instead, her lips curling slightly as she considered his well-muscled black torso and other well-developed areas.

By eleven-thirty that evening there was still no news from Adam Beckford and the technical support team had received no further signals from the tracking devices. The ransom had been taken, but neither Lorraine Girding nor

Eve Beckford had been released. There would have to be a press release tomorrow; matters had gone too far now.

20

"C'mon, Sir, it's pointless just driving around aimlessly," Karen Preece moaned. "We need a change of scenery. Let's find a wine-bar somewhere and try and generate some new ideas."

"It's gone time," Parlour replied dully.

"We're halfway to Foxburgh now. There's a bistro with extended opening hours as you drive in on this road. I've been there with the Sewer once."

"Must have been pleasant for you," Parlour grinned, thinking of the late, and rather flatulent, Detective Chief Inspector. Parlour had taken his office on promotion to DCI - following a thorough going over by the industrial cleaners.

"So it takes a mention of DCI Fartpants to bring a smile to your face, then?" Preece laughed.

"I'll chill out a bit as soon as we get some kind of lead on this damn case," Parlour stated more soberly this time. "I can't believe we haven't had a single scrap of useful information from the public about the whereabouts of these women. Does the whole world walk around with earphones in and their heads up their bums?"

"That's some mean feat," Preece grinned.

"Or maybe it's a case of *See No Evil, Hear No Evil*," Parlour mused. "Well someone's got to give the game away soon."

"You hope," Preece grunted.

Within fifteen minutes, they had found a secluded spot boasting a black leather sofa at the far end of *Kick-Back*, a rather soul-less wine-bar/bistro with challenging lighting. At least they wouldn't be spotted together, Parlour thought to himself dryly; a bat would struggle in these conditions.

"The usual?" Parlour enquired, checking his wallet for the ten pound note he would undoubtedly require at an establishment such as this. Preece nodded and Parlour proceeded to the bar to purchase a red wine Spritze for his colleague and a low alcohol lager for himself.

"Mark Parlour, you never cease to surprise me!"

Parlour turned at the bar to look up into the eyes of Desiree Lamarr, a prominent defence lawyer of national repute whom Parlour had bumped into at various court cases over the years. He smiled at the willowy lady, clearly off duty in a little red number that accentuated her breathtakingly long legs.

"Didn't except to see you in a place like this! Thought your lot frequented *The Pig and Whistle*?"

"Trying a change of scenery to bolster the old grey cells," Parlour smiled, then gave his order to a well-dressed young man behind the bar. "And it's *The Coach and Whistle*."

"Chasing down any mass murderers at the moment, then?" Desiree grinned, glass of something fizzy and expensive in her hand.

"Could be," Parlour replied cagily, pocketing the minimal change from a ten pound note. He exchanged a few more pleasantries before making his way back to Karen Preece with the drinks.

"Who's Venus Williams?" Karen asked. Even the dimmest of lighting could not obscure that red dress and *those* legs.

"Desiree Lamarr."

"Desiree Lamarr?" Preece echoed, nearly spitting out her drink. "Didn't she win X-Factor or something?"

"Actually, she's a lawyer, Karen. And a darn handy one, at that."

"The type that just names her price," Preece commented, considering the leggy young woman across the room from them.

"I'd say so, yes," Parlour nodded, sipping at his unleaded beer.

"How come I've never come across her, then?" Preece wondered.

"Foxburgh Crown Court is my second home, don't you know!"

Parlour laughed and patted Preece's shoulder. "You won't see Desiree Lamarr in this neck of the woods. She's top drawer, works for the CPS."

"So how come she consorts with the likes of you, *boss*," Preece grinned, not without a small degree of flirty coyness.

"Oh, I got invited to some Police Awards shindig in London a few years back," Parlour replied dismissively. "She was sat at my table."

"Bet she's got a queue of men a mile long chasing after her," Preece stated, though without envy.

"I think she probably scares most of them witless," Parlour replied, characteristically eschewing an opportune occasion to swear.

"Does she scare you?" Preece enquired, a twinkle in her dark eyes.

Parlour smiled. "She's a little intimidating, being so tall, I guess. But it's irrelevant, in any case. She's taken."

"Married?"

Parlour nodded.

"She looks too young," Preece frowned, screwing up her eyes to get a better view of her across the dimly lit room.

"She's in her thirties," Parlour stated. "She's older than she looks."

"So who's the lucky man?"

"Des is married to a copper, actually," Parlour replied, sitting back on the sofa and resting his feet on the tip of the low level drinks table. "Some guy in CID from Thames Valley. Fox, I think. Never met him; might be on secondment from the Met, think he's quite new there. They live in Reading – not sure what she's doing down here. Some kind of hen celebration, by the looks of it." Parlour considered the giggly party of women across the room from them.

"Did you say Fox?" Preece checked, trying to keep her voice steady.

"That's right. She never changed her name – for professional reasons, probably. Mind you, would you change your name to common old Fox if you had a surname like hers?"

But Preece was barely listening. *Fox,* Preece thought to herself. *Sly Fox. Bloody lying cheating Fox.*

"Do you know him?" Parlour enquired.

"Might have bumped into him once or twice - on a course, I think," Preece replied thinly. She got up. "Just nipping to the loo."

"OK." Parlour watched her back. Had he said something? He was distracted from ruminating further on Preece's sudden departure by the realisation that he had forgotten to inform Juliet of his late return that evening. Parlour flipped open his mobile and called home. But the signal was poor; he would try again later.

She's a long time, Parlour thought, when Karen Preece still hadn't appeared after a few minutes. He picked up his drink and ambled over to where Desiree Lamarr was giggling raucously with her entourage. It had been a stressful day and Karen was not proving the best of company that evening. Parlour conveniently forgot that he had himself been like a bear with a hangover these past few weeks.

"So what's the occasion?" he grinned, once Desiree had introduced him to the dozen or so ladies aged between 25 and 40. The jaw-droppingly gorgeous lawyer explained that one of the girls, an old college friend of Desiree's, was leaving the Hampshire legal firm where she was based to travel the world.

"I'm very envious," Parlour conceded. "Now that I've become a father, getting out of the front door in the morning is an achievement in itself!"

"I intend having at least five years of fun with Shaun before I get myself laden with a kiddie," Desiree replied, laughing.

"Can we go now, boss?" Karen Preece asked, interrupting the jollities.

"Karen! I didn't see you there," Parlour turned and faced his DI, noticing a puffiness around her eyes immediately. He steered her away from the crowd.

"What's up?"

"Can we please just get out of here?" Preece pleaded desperately.

Parlour nodded, and returning to grab their coats, left *Kick-Back*. Suddenly he had an inkling of what may be up with his junior colleague. Parlour had the good sense to say nothing until they were back on the road. He pulled up in a lay-by back on the road towards Billock Station.

"That friend in Reading... was it by any chance Shaun Fox?" His eyes bore into her cheek as she stared straight ahead, willing herself not to cry.

What's wrong with me, crying over some stupid eedjit man, Preece berated herself silently. *Come on, you're made of stronger stuff than this!*

She simply nodded. A tear escaped her furious attempts to blink it back and rolled down her sparsely fleshed cheek.

"How did you guess?"

Parlour shrugged. "Moment of inspiration?"

He laid a comforting hand on her denim clad leg. Preece winced at his touch and turned to face his concerned gaze. "Sorry boss."

"He obviously made quite an impression on you," Parlour stated quietly, a flurry of mixed emotions fluttering in his brain. Whilst he could not deny he felt triumphant that Karen Preece was no longer likely to pursue a relationship with this Shaun Fox character, he regretted her suffering and could not help but spare a thought for Desiree Lamarr, blissfully unaware that her sparkling new marriage was a sham. Perhaps there was some truth in the claim that money and success couldn't buy you happiness, after all.

"Come here," Parlour said gently, extending his arm and pulling Karen into his body. He squeezed her as tightly to him as he could, insofar as was possible with a gear-stick and handbrake between them.

"I knew there was something suss about him," Preece snuffled into his chest. "He said so little about himself beyond shop talk - and as for that ridiculous shag pad of his..."

"Spare me, Karen," Parlour hushed her, "I don't want to know."

"I'm sorry, I forget you're a squeaky clean married man," Preece sniffed, withdrawing her head from Parlour's chest, but not resisting when he immediately pulled it back there.

"It's not that," Parlour said quietly, stroking her short black hair. Preece squeezed her eyes shut, hoping Parlour could not feel her heart thumping against her chest wall.

"What then?" Karen asked finally after a very long and very loud silence.

"Nothing," Parlour said shortly, thinking guiltily of his wife and child lying asleep at home.

"Poor Des Lamarr," he said instead. "Guess she has no idea her new husband's a philandering son of a..."

"I feel such an idiot," Preece stated, wiping her eyes with the back of her hand and pulling her head away. She gave Parlour a watery smile.

"Thanks boss... Mark. You won't..."

"Shaun who?" Parlour grinned. As the moon peeped out through the clouds and illuminated the front of Parlour's silver car, his facial expression intensified into an unmistakeable look of desire. He stretched a hand out and gently pulled Preece's chin towards him.

Karen Preece did not resist as Parlour's lips rested on hers, then tentatively explored her mouth. Ignoring the vibration in his front left pocket, a timely reminder of his marital status,

Parlour forgot about his wife's incoming call as Preece responded to his kiss. She began to rake her slender hand through her senior colleague's auburn hair, her other hand about to release them from the confines of their outer garments before both were blinded by the headlights of a squad car pulling up behind them.

With an almighty shove, Parlour pushed his colleague away from him and hissed at her to sit up and stay in the car. Straightening his clothes, he alighted from the vehicle.

Parlour uttered a silent prayer of thanksgiving, realising it was PC Jason Malkins, a quiet lad who had joined the force last year, and his usual sidekick, PC Nick Clough, another lad who kept his head down and got on with the job in hand.

"Ah, Sir, didn't realise it was you," PC Malkins smiled, getting out of the car from the passenger's side. "Been told to keep an eye out in the area, you know, for the kidnappers of..."

"Yes, Jason, I am the SIO on the Girding/Beckford case," Parlour responded rather testily, heart thumping as he assessed how much damage limitation was required. It was not a situation in which he had ever found himself before, and not one he wished ever to repeat. What on earth had got into him?

"Er, well, sorry to bother you, Sir, I'll just.. er.."

"I stopped to brief a colleague, Jason," Parlour informed him hastily. "I was just on my way back to the Station, anyway."

"Right you are, Sir," Malkins smiled politely and walked backwards to the car, as if taking leave of Royalty.

De-brief, more like, Malkins thought to himself, smirking at his own joke.

Parlour slammed the car door shut and drove off with as much dignity as he could muster, before putting his foot down once the squad car was out of sight in his rear view mirror. Neither of them said a word all the way back to Billock Station.

21

Tuesday 15 November 2011

It had been a long time since Parlour had woken up with that dreadful sinking feeling that weighs down all respectable people the morning after a major loss of control. And the sensation was all the worse for his being twenty years older this time, and compounded by the sheer idiocy of what had nearly transpired between Karen Preece and himself.

"You might have called me last night," Juliet grumbled, as Parlour sat up wearily in bed, squinting as his eyes adjusted to the lamplight. "It's not like you to ignore my calls."

"I'm sorry, Jules," Parlour apologised, clearing his throat. "The signal was bad, then I was up to my eyes in the kidnappings."

He was a poor liar.

"They haven't returned either of the women, have they?"

"How do you know that?" Parlour frowned, slipping into his dressing gown and making his way towards the en-suite bathroom. Surely the Super wouldn't have approved a press release without his consent?

"You came back last night," Juliet stated matter-of-factly. "You'd have been up all night questioning the women and following up leads if they'd been released."

"There are no flies on you, are there?" Parlour stated listlessly, contemplating his troublesome complexion in the bathroom mirror.

"So what's next?" Juliet called through.

"Guess we'll need to issue a press release before any more women are abducted," Parlour replied miserably. "We were staving off until we were sure the two cases were linked, but the ransom notes prove they are."

"So will you mention the wacky notes?"

"Not sure yet. Need to discuss with the Super how much info to release."

So preoccupied was Parlour with the events of the previous evening, that he neglected to enquire what Juliet's plans for the day were, as was his usual custom. Juliet was relieved, uncomfortable at the prospect of lying to her husband concerning the sudden appearance of a week's worth of groceries in the kitchen cupboards.

Parlour could not fault either Karen Preece's professionalism or her dedication to the job. It would have been far easier to have called in sick and avoided him that morning, but there she was, tapping away furiously on the computer as if her life depended on it, phone handset nestled between her ear and shoulder.

Parlour slipped past her and walked noiselessly into his office.

"Oh, hello, Sir," he stated, rather taken aback to find Superintendent Dewhurst waiting for him in his own leather chair.

"I won't beat around the bush, Parlour," Dewhurst said gruffly. "We've heard neither hide nor hair of our kidnapper friends and there's no sign of the banknotes. The door to door enquiries have proven a dead loss. In short, we're completely stuffed. We need to get a press release out before another woman mysteriously disappears into thin air."

"How about a reward for info leading to their whereabouts?" Parlour proposed.

"Maybe BestCo will do us a year's supply of Bran Flakes," Dewhurst grunted, grabbing Parlour's desk as leverage to hoist his bulky frame from the chair. "But make it Kellogg's, none of that value muck. Can you get Beckford and Girding over here for a conflab asap. And get Lynda Miles up here, too."

Lynda Miles was Billock Police Station's press officer.

"Will do," Parlour nodded and shut the door behind the retreating back of Detective Superintendent Dewhurst.

Parlour gave the room a quick blast of air freshener then pulled his little black leather book from his top drawer. The page conveniently fell open at Psalm 51 and King David repenting of his adultery with Bathsheba. He groaned and shoved his Bible back in the drawer. He rested his temples on his fingers and prayed for forgiveness with the urgency of the severely troubled.

Karen Preece lifted a hand to tap gently on the door, but seeing Parlour lost in his thoughts, thought better of it and returned to her desk.

***

With the resigned approval of Robert Girding and Adam Beckford, Billock CID issued a televised press release at 12.30 pm, informing the public of the abduction of Lorraine Girding and Eve Beckford, and appealing for any information, however trivial it might seem, that may aid the police in their enquiries.

It was a risky undertaking, given the contents of the ransom note warning against police involvement. However, the threat to housewives all over the county posed by the phantom doorstep snatchers could not be ignored; therefore Superintendent Dewhurst and the Chief Constable of Billock Police made the decision to run with the appeal. Billock CID was already visibly involved in the investigation, in any case; in Dewhurst's view, this was a calculated risk worth taking. As he put it to Parlour in typically blunt fashion, the women would already be dead if the abductors kept to their word, as the kidnappers had clearly intimated knowledge of the police surveillance unit set up the first ransom handover and of attempts to track the banknotes.

It was a quiet day for news, and BBC South went live to the appeal. It was broadcast simultaneously on Radio Solent as well as other local radio stations. The housewives of Billock and surrounding areas were warned not to open their doors to strangers until the abductors were apprehended. In the unlikely event that the kidnappers should strike again in the same area following the press release, details of the unusual ransom request were also made public.

Shortly after twelve-thirty pm, David Sheffrey, a delivery driver for BestCo online grocery service, rang on the doorbell of a smart four bed property in Spatchcock Drive, Deverton. There was no answer. Sheffrey tried again, but still no signs of adult life.

Sheffrey frowned. There was a car in the driveway and he could hear a baby crying inside. Perhaps Mum was on the loo or something. Sheffrey returned to the delivery van and fetched his mobile phone. If Mrs Juliet Parlour didn't come to the door in a minute, he'd try her on the landline. Perhaps the doorbell wasn't working, or she had the vacuum cleaner on upstairs. There was usually a practical explanation for such occurrences.

Sheffrey quickly poked his head above the locked side gate, but there was no sign of the elusive Mrs Parlour in the back garden, either. He called out, in case she was hanging out washing in an area unseen from his vantage point. But no reply. When a third assault on the doorbell yielded no results, Sheffrey tried the landline, squinting in the late autumn sun to read the numbers from the computer printout of her grocery order. He heard the phone ringing inside, but he hung up as the answer phone clicked in. He'd try the mobile number supplied, but if there was no reply on that, he'd have no option but to leave a message and try again later. It was a bit worrying about that baby, though. What if Mum had taken ill, or fallen down the stairs and knocked herself out and that poor baby was stuck inside, helpless?

Uneasy, Sheffrey tried the front door handle, but it was one of those ultra secure double-glazed types that couldn't be opened from the outside without a key. The chunky padlock on the side gate would take some handiwork to destroy, and

Shreffrey didn't feel he ought to attempt it in any case. Neither did the gate provide any purchase to enable Shreffrey to climb over and try the back door.

There were no cars in the driveways on either side of the property; it looked like the neighbours were out. He could hardly leave her groceries with a neighbour, but they might at least have some idea of where Mrs Parlour may have got to. Sheffrey knocked on a few neighbouring doors, but there wasn't a soul about. Shreffrey left a message on both the land-line and mobile number, then perplexed, called the delivery manager back at base.

22

"So what now?" DS Cameron Goodlove enquired, leaning his elbows on the canteen table as Parlour joined him for a coffee. Parlour had been chained to his desk all morning, dealing with the press and sifting and re-sifting through the information collated by the murder enquiry team he'd assembled. It was a relief to escape from the Perspex box that was his office and - it had to be said - from Karen Preece. He felt vibes of tension travelling - almost in waves – from her desk through the partition wall. She was studiously avoiding him, yet the critical point at which the murder enquiry was balanced required that she remained very much within the hub of activity. Personal issues had to be cast aside in pursuit of the common goal of delivering Lorraine Girding and Eve Beckford safely back to their families.

"I guess all we can do is wait and hope that Joe Public has spotted something untoward and gets in touch," Parlour shrugged, looking - in Goodlove's view - thoroughly defeated.

"So what happened with the tracking devices?" Goodlove frowned. "Tech Support reckoned these things are so small, they'd never have spotted them."

"If they're a professional outfit, they'd have ways and means," Parlour replied soberly. "Or they've left the bag of notes still submersed in water to stop us tracking them."

"You can't get a signal through water, right?"

"No," Parlour confirmed. "They probably dumped the bag in a top-box full of water, if they were on two wheels. Or in a cool box of sorts, if they were in a car."

"They're not amateurs, then?"

Parlour screwed up his face. "I wouldn't go that far. A weekly dose of all the police procedurals and forensic police series on the box can give your average Joe plenty top tips on concealing evidence."

"'Spose," Goodlove conceded. There was a brief pause as the two men sipped at their hot coffees.

"Do you think we were right not to bring in a surveillance unit this time?" Goodlove pondered, playing with the sugar sachets in a pot on the table, a habit that infuriated the pernickety Parlour.

"You can't play with people's lives, Cam," Parlour stated, more than a little pompously. He shook his head, then looked up and met his DS in the eye. "You have no idea how terrible I felt when Lorraine Girding wasn't released, and we got that dire warning from the kidnappers. Anyway, it was Adam Beckford's request that we took this approach, when I ran through all the options with him."

"Do you think they'll strike again?"

Parlour weighed it up in his mind. "I just don't know. I'd like to think they'll quit while they're ahead, now we've warned the public. Hopefully they'll take the money and run, leaving our two women alive if not exactly kicking. But I really couldn't say for sure which way it'll go."

Goodlove frowned. "I reckon they'll be worried the women squeal. I think we'll be lucky to find them alive, very lucky."

"A double murder charge is quite different from abduction," Parlour responded. "Though you're talking a custodial sentence for abduction, it's definitely life for double murder. Depends how confident they are of getting away with it. By now they could be out of the country, £100k to the good. We may have put all the ports on alert, but that doesn't mean they didn't slip through the net."

"There's something bothering me, though, boss," Goodlove frowned.

"What's that?"

"Well, £50k isn't exactly a life-changing amount. Why not ask for more, or choose a more affluent victim?"

"That has bothered me, I admit, Cam," Parlour replied. "And I've already had that conversation with the boss this morning. I think they knew £50k was the sort of amount the likes of successful middle class professionals like Girding and Beckford could afford to lose at an absolute push. Much more, and fulfilling the ransom request would have been a no-no. As to why they didn't pick on the filthy rich... my guess is it's a question of access. Given the complete lack of sightings of either women on the day of their abduction, the most likely scenario is that they were kidnapped from their own homes. Try ringing on the doorbell of the average celebrity from OK! Magazine – you wouldn't even get past the electric gates, let alone manage to snatch a woman on her own doorstep."

"And the motive?"

Parlour shrugged. "Drugs? Sex? Pay off the mortgage? Your guess is as good as mine. Perhaps there's some personal grudge involved that we've yet to uncover."

They were interrupted at that point by the arrival of Sean Denton. He handed Parlour a mobile phone.

"I guess this is yours, boss? It's been ringing non-stop, thought it might be your missus or something, trying to get hold of you."

"Thanks, Sean," Parlour nodded, taking his Blackberry from Denton and flicking to *missed calls.*

"It's not Jules," he frowned, not recognising the entry. He wandered over to the canteen window and dialled the unknown number.

"Everything alright, boss?" Goodlove checked, as Parlour returned to the table and put his suit jacket on, which had been draped over the back of the plastic chair.

"That was BestCo over at the industrial estate," Parlour replied, brow furrowed. "Apparently Juliet ordered a home delivery of shopping – not that she told me about it – but they've turned up and she's not answering the door."

"Maybe she forgot to stay in for them," Goodlove shrugged. "It's easily done. In fact, I'm surprised Sainsbury haven't banned me for life, I've done it that often."

"They can hear the baby crying, but she's not coming to the door. And she's not answering the landline or her mobile, either."

"On the loo?"

"For an hour?" Parlour exclaimed. "The driver went off and did a few more deliveries and returned, but she still didn't come to the door – and he could still hear Rowan crying! I have to go home – can you let Dewhurst and Karen know?"

"Bloody hell," Goodlove whistled, as Parlour dashed off in the direction of the staff car park.

"What's up with him?" Denton enquired, returning from the servery with a lukewarm plate of beef curry on a bed of luminous saffron rice. Goodlove filled him in on the details.

"Think she's..." Denton began.

Goodlove held his hand up. "Don't even go there. She's probably nodded off – judging by the state of old Pizza's skin at the moment, don't think the pair of them are getting much R&R at the mo."

"Is that what they call it these days?" Denton snickered flippantly.

Across the canteen, PC Jason Malkins sat opposite his colleague Nick Clough, who was pouring over the football editorial in that day's paper.

"You know what I thought I saw last night?"

"You mean old Pizza getting his end away?" Clough grinned, shovelling a forkful of undercooked bacon into his mouth.

"Don't say a word to anyone. I'm not sure I saw anything really, and it could really eff up his career – he's a good bloke."

"Who was he with, anyway?" Clough frowned, sweeping his fried bread around in the egg yolk with his fork.

"Looked like that skinny bird in CID. The new DI."

"Karen something," Clough nodded. "Rees? Rice? Price? Katie Price?"

"Hardly!" Malkins scoffed. "Anyway, I saw her this morning. Looked really rough, like she'd been crying."

"Maybe Pizza was just comforting her or something," Malkins stated, tucking into a jacket potato overflowing with baked beans.

"Thought you said he was giving her one," Clough grinned.

"I didn't see that much," Malkins conceded. "But he definitely had his arms round some bird, and it looked like her."

"She could've had some bad news," Clough shrugged. "Like you say, best forget about it. Pizza's a decent bloke, don't really think he would cheat on that sexy missus of his – even if she has blobbed out a bit."

Malkins nodded and steered the conversation back to the weekend's football fixtures.

23

"You can go now, but thanks for waiting for me," Parlour told the anxious BestCo delivery driver, who, despite finishing his shift early and returning the delivery van to the depot, had decided to return to Spatchcock Drive in his own car to keep watch on the house. David Shreffrey, a grey-haired benign-faced man of around fifty, scuttled up the driveway after Parlour.

"My daughter has a baby; I'd be worried sick if I thought something had happened to her and the nipper was left to fend for itself."

"You've been brilliant, thanks so much," Parlour said breathlessly, slotting his key into the lock. *You'll win Online Grocery Delivery Driver of the Year*, don't you worry. He swore, realising Juliet had left her key in the other side, and that he was therefore unable to unlock the front door. He undid the padlock on the side gate and accessed the house via the back door instead.

"I said you can go now!" Parlour barked at the rather shocked delivery driver, who beat a retreat to his car on the roadside, but no further. Heart thumping and feeling sick to the pit of his stomach, Parlour picked up a beetroot and soggy Rowan from his baby bouncer in the living room and tore through the house, the infant continuing to screech in his arms as Parlour flung open the garage door in vain.

It can't be true, no no no no no! Parlour was sobbing now, great heaving sobs that hurt his diaphragm as he saw his wife's keys in the lock and her handbag on the hall table, mobile phone poking out of a side compartment. Her car was still parked on the driveway; just like Lorraine Girding's had been.

He checked the answer phone. There was the usual sleep-inducing message from her parents, then two messages from BestCo. The first was from the clearly worried delivery driver, enquiring whether Mrs Parlour was at home to receive her shopping, the second from the supermarket's Delivery Manager, checking that Mrs Parlour was OK and requesting a call back to arrange redelivery of her groceries.

Parlour checked his wife's mobile. There were two almost identical messages from BestCo plus a missed call from Kate D'Archeville, an old college pal of Juliet's that Parlour had met a couple of times. Nothing odd in that, he decided, except that he would have expected her to call Juliet on the land-line.

Taking a deep breath, he dialled Billock CID. As fate would have it, he was put through to DI Karen Preece.

Preece arrived in Spatchcock Drive within fifteen minutes. Determined to get there ahead of the crew so that she could have a quick word with her boss, Preece had driven at breakneck speed to Parlour's place in Deverton. She was still suffering from a dull headache from the night before, having drowned her sorrows in the trusty company of Jack Daniels on return to her two bedroom flat in Billock. But what was a bad head and a guilty conscience compared to the hellish situation in which her colleague now found himself? It was necessary to draw a quick line under the previous evening and move on, for Juliet Parlour's sake, if nothing else.

"Hi, Karen," Parlour said hollowly, opening the front door to her.

"Where's Rowan?"

"Upstairs," Parlour replied flatly, indicating with his head in the direction of the stairwell. "Screamed himself to sleep – finally. Amazing what a clean nappy and a bottle of formula can do."

Preece nodded, then taking his arm, pulled him into the front room. "Boss – Mark. About last night..."

Parlour turned away, but Preece grabbed his arm again and forced him to meet her in the eye.

"I was tired; I was upset and angry about that bastard Fox, and the wine went to my head. You were knackered and probably haven't had a shag in ages. It was just a physical...

biological... whatever... reaction to circumstances. Just forget about it. We work well together, we have to work well together – for Juliet and Rowan's sake. So just get over it – now. That's what I told myself the moment the call came in. I just felt we needed to get that out of the way first."

Parlour nodded miserably, his mind elsewhere. As he stood trembling, Preece longed to wrap her arms around him, but in the circumstances, resisted and instead adopted a firm tone of voice.

"So her car's in the driveway, you say the keys were in the lock, and her purse and mobile are still here."

Parlour confirmed this was true and sank down on the sofa, head in his hands, as Preece opened the door to Superintendent Dewhurst.

"Parlour," Dewhurst announced, mopping his shiny red forehead with a once white handkerchief. "I'm taking over as SIO on this one – I'm sure you understand why. Preece here will remain in the Incident Room, gathering and analysing incoming information. Futile I know, telling you to butt out, so I'm sending you out with Goodlove on the door to doors and following other leads. Keep you busy, best thing for you. You'll be able to sort out childcare for the little fella?"

Parlour nodded miserably, realising the hysterical fit that would follow when he informed Juliet's parents - as he would have to - that their daughter had been abducted by, at best, a serial abductor and at worst, a potential serial killer.

"Thank you, Sir," he said, realising Dewhurst was completely within his rights to take Parlour off the case entirely on the grounds of conflict of interests.

"You understand, of course, Parlour, that strict procedure must be followed at all times, even if your wife *is* involved. No buggering off half-cock."

"Naturally," Parlour muttered, still wondering how on God's earth he was going to break the news to the in-laws.

As Parlour disappeared to make the necessary call to Derek and Margaret Hebble, Dewhurst took a crumpled piece of paper from his inside pocket.

"Beckford received this in the post this morning. I've made a copy from the bagged original – that's why it's a bit tricky to read."

He handed the sheet of A4 to Preece, who scanned it quickly. It was written in the same bland Times New Roman script.

Cute, but not cute enough! Tell your police mates to ditch the trackers and the women go free!

"It's just a ruse," Preece stated, shaking her head. "The bastards have no intention of letting the women go until they've made their two hundred k – or whatever it is they're after."

"Do you think they know they've nabbed Parlour's missus this time?" Dewhurst wondered.

"You definitely think it's the same gang at work?" Preece checked, playing devil's advocate.

Dewhurst made a *Cum'offit* face and hastily stuffed the photocopy back in his pocket before Parlour made a re-entry. "Bleedin' obviously is, wouldn't you say, Karen?"

"Unfortunately, yes," Preece nodded soberly. "Same MO. So do you think they've targeted Parlour's wife, then?"

"Do you?"

Tossing the verbal ball back was one of Superintendent Dewhurst's most annoying habits, performed, Preece and co were sure, to make him sound supercilious and superior and to prevent him, by default, from drawing any false conclusions for which he may be held accountable.

Preece frowned. "Not sure. It would be a far riskier strategy, from their point of view – I wouldn't tell the public this, but we're naturally going to double our efforts to find the abductor of the spouse of one of our own boys. I think it's a coincidence. Juliet Parlour obviously fits the type of woman they're targeting. She doesn't work, she has a child, her husband is perceived to be successful and they have a nice house. They don't realise the relatively humble salary of a DCI – which suggests to me, they don't know who Mark Parlour is. I would have been surprised if DCI Parlour has a spare £50k knocking about to pay a ransom note."

Dewhurst flapped his hand in a derisory fashion. "There are ways around that, Preece. However, that's a pretty fair assessment, I'd say."

"How was it?" Preece asked, as Parlour entered the room, ashen-faced.

"Not good," Parlour replied quietly. "I'm taking Rowan round to the in-laws. I guess this place is out of bounds till the CSOs have been and checked for prints."

"Take Karen here with you, Parlour. You've had a nasty shock."

"No... I'd rather be by myself, thank you... Sir," Parlour said hastily, avoiding Preece's concerned gaze.

***

"What was the name of that copper?" The beefy lad with the shaven head enquired, swerving a white van onto the hard shoulder of the M275.

"Parlour, I think – as in Massage," a skinny lad with multiple piercings chortled. "What's the problem, Jez? Why've you suddenly pulled over?"

"Are you deaf as well as dumb?" The character named Jez exclaimed.

"That was a press release about the women. The Senior Investigating Officer, you know, the bloke in charge of the case, was called something Parlour, I'm sure of it."

"And?"

120

"*And,* you numpty, number 3 in the back here's called Parlour, ain't she?"

Jez indicated with his thumb in a backwards direction towards the caged off rear, where a drugged Juliet Parlour lay foetal-like on an old rag. Parlour's wife was surrounded by electrical cables and other paraphernalia associated with the electrician's trade; this was the profession Jez and Paul practised in their spare time, when not currying favour for assorted undesirables from the local criminal underworld.

"Dunno – is she?" Paul grabbed Juliet Parlour's contact details handed to them earlier by the boss and groaned.

Jez blasphemed loudly and threw his mobile phone at his skinny accomplice. "Phone the Guv, I need to get off the hard shoulder before the Old Bill pull up and start asking questions."

24

"Where's Parlour?" Detective Superintendent Dewhurst frowned at Preece, as she returned to the Incident Room, ham salad sandwich and a bottled Smoothie in hand. He couldn't pretend to be happy at the thought of a desperation-fuelled Parlour roaming the streets in search of his wife, but knew there was no point trying to take Parlour completely off the case. At least this way, he was accompanied by Goodlove. Dewhurst knew that if the tables were turned, and his beloved Fran had been abducted, he would feel exactly the same as Parlour.

"Driving around the county rattling the doors of lock-ups and garage blocks. He's convinced the women are being held somewhere locally. We've already combed the area, but you know what he's like – and what sort of frame of mind he must be in."

"Poor sod," Dewhurst commiserated. "So what have you got for me?"

"We've exhausted the immediate area around his house, Sir. Nobody within sight of Spatchcock Drive, who was actually in at the time, noticed a strange vehicle calling there, or anywhere else in the street. Not a very nosey bunch around there - heads up their bums, most of them. There was only one house that views directly onto Mark's house where the neighbours weren't at work. They confirmed that they saw a blue BestCo van pull up but thought nothing of it as they often see supermarket delivery vans in the area – though usually Utopia vans, admittedly, in that neck of the woods."

"But it pulled up several times and the delivery man got out and called over the fence," Dewhurst frowned.

"They only noticed it the first time, at around 12.35pm," Preece replied, consulting her notepad. "The lady of the house, a Mrs Joyce Beverley, said she was busy in the back garden with her husband – they're retired - and had popped in to make coffee. She saw the van pull up from her kitchen window and saw the driver call at the door. She was distracted by the phone ringing and left the kitchen, so didn't see anything else."

"And that's all she told you – no other vans, no other vehicles?"

"That's all I've got," Preece confirmed, shaking her head. "Not much return for a morning's graft."

"OK. Can you assemble the rest of the team in here? If I'm taking over this case, I need to find out exactly where we'll all at in this investigation."

"What about Parlour, Sir?"

"Leave him out for the minute. It'll be easier to talk without him here and he's probably not within shouting distance, anyway."

"OK, boss," Preece replied somewhat uneasily. Though the situation was unprecedented at Billock CID, Parlour still very much needed to be there, in her view. He had a far better grasp of the investigation so far than Dewhurst, and given that his own wife had been abducted, he more than any other member of the team needed to be kept abreast of every single development. Preece made a mental note to call Parlour the moment the meeting had ended and fill him in on the state of play.

Within ten minutes, eight of the twelve strong team from CID investigating the abductions, plus two of the technical support team, were sat in front of the interactive white board in the Incident Room. Goodlove had remained at Parlour's side.

Dewhurst began by recapping on the circumstances surrounding the kidnappings of Lorraine Girding and Eve Beckford. He pointed out the similarities between the lifestyles of the two ladies but that, despite exhaustive searches, no common ground could be found between either the two ladies, or their spouses. There was no history between either couple as far as could be ascertained. In both cases, the door to door enquiries had generated no leads on the two abductions, though tyre marks in the gravel outside the Girdings' residence suggested a large van had pulled up at the door recently. Forensics had done a thorough search of the ransom drop-off point and had found tyre prints from an off-road type motorcycle.

"No sightings of the bike, I take it?" Dewhurst asked gloomily.

Sean Denton shook his head. "No public sightings of any motorcyclists, and no abandoned motorcycles in the area. The ransom collector most likely drove straight into the back of a van and made their getaway that way, as the tyre tracks peter out where the scrubland meets the road."

"These types of bikes have quite a distinctive sound, though, don't they?" Dewhurst persevered. "Bit like a fly trapped behind the curtains."

"Again, he or she probably got off the bike once they were out of the woods," Denton replied.

"And nothing from the ports or airports?"

Preece shook her head. "Customs have reported no suspicious activity in relation to this enquiry."

"What about the phone-lines? Any new information since the appeal was broadcast?"

"Nothing of use, Sir," Preece shook her head. "But it's early days yet."

"And as for Mrs Parlour," Dewhurst began respectfully, turning his attention to the latest abduction. "I understand that yet again, the neighbours have nothing to declare? This is beginning to feel like a bleedin' conspiracy!"

"Just the way of the world, these days," Preece shrugged. "People don't want to raise their head above the parapet, even if they have seen something. It's not worth it – you get some nutter reeking revenge on your house or kids. Think of that poor bloke in Warrington who dared to stand up to a bunch of teenage nuisances. But to be fair, in all three cases, there's been hardly anyone at home in the streets in question. The majority of women work these days, and most retired people have social lives to match your average university fresher!"

"Any news from the lab on fingerprints?"

Preece shook her head. "No foreign prints on or around the door frame. Reckon the abductor wore gloves."

"So why Juliet Parlour?" Dewhurst asked. He pointed to her image, blown up from the family photo on Parlour's desk.

There was resounding silence.

"To cock a snook at DCI Parlour?" Denton proposed, more for the sake of saying something, than from genuine conviction.

"In what way?" Dewhurst pushed him.

"To mock him - to mock us all - that we haven't caught up with them yet."

"It's possible," Dewhurst conceded. "But they would have to have inside knowledge to know that Parlour was the SIO on this one – up until now. Juliet Parlour was abducted before we issued the press release at twelve-thirty, giving Parlour as the point of contact."

"True," Denton agreed. "The boss has been on telly before though. He's pretty well-known since he put the Paraquat Poisoner away."

"You still wouldn't assume he was the SIO on this case, though. And whilst you might recognise Parlour to look at with his carrot top and his... erm... dermatological difficulties, would you really remember his name from something that happened in the news two years ago? I don't think so."

"Unless it was someone connected with that case," Preece interjected.

"Pretty bloody unlikely," Dewhurst snorted derisorily.

"I reckon it was pure coincidence," Preece commented. "There's some link between the three women, maybe something glaringly obvious, that we're just not spotting. Something stupid, like they've all given personal details to the same mail order company or something. Someone somewhere knows that these three women would be at home alone and seized their chance."

"I think Karen is right," Dewhurst nodded slowly. He slammed the desk in front of him with his porky hand. "Damn it! I just cannot believe we don't have a single lead on who took these women!"

"Is there any chance our delivery driver isn't quite who he says he is?"

Denton frowned. "Remember that other case Parlour solved in Deverton, with the bogus postman?"

"What do you mean?" Dewhurst barked.

"Well, Sir, we only have Dave Sheffrey's word for it that he tried to deliver Mrs Parlour's shopping. Maybe he abducted her in his van, took her to wherever they're holding the other two women, then returned, pretending to redeliver the shopping."

"Storing her precisely where in transit, Denton?" Dewhurst snorted. "In the freezer compartment? Have you seen the inside of one of those vans?"

"It's not a totally outlandish idea, Sir," Preece defended her colleague. "And we only have a sighting of the outside of the van, not its internal fittings. However, we've already checked with BestCo, and they did indeed receive contact from David Sheffrey at the times he told us he rang them. We've asked them to fax over a phone log and they're going to fax over Juliet Parlour's internet order, as well. What's more, David Sheffrey is a much treasured delivery driver – a bit of a housewife's favourite, by all accounts. The Alan Titchmarsh of Online Grocery Shopping. He's squeaky clean – and by alerting us so soon, may end up being a hero after all."

"Emphasis on *may*, Preece," Dewhurst grunted. "OK. We need to keep manning those phones and hope Joe Public turns up trumps. Meanwhile, can somebody give Parlour a bell and tell him to return home. He might just spot something missing or out of place that could give us a clue as to what the hell is going on. He can also provide us with information about Mrs

Parlour's shopping habits. I reckon Karen's idea, that something impersonal links these three women, is our best bet at the moment."

"Shouldn't we check with Robert Girding and Adam Beckford, to see whether their wives used BestCo as well?" Sean Denton enquired.

"I tell you, that delivery man is as clean as a whistle!" Dewhurst exclaimed.

"Play golf with him, Sir?" Karen Preece grinned.

Only she could get away with that, Sean Denton thought to himself, noting how both Dewhurst and Parlour fawned over the newly promoted Detective Inspector. She was the type of women that older men went nuts for – smart, ballsy, slightly boyish yet feminine enough to be sexy. And occasionally, albeit only very occasionally, the smart cookie crumbled a little, revealing a vulnerability that reduced them to a simpering puddle on the floor.

"B!" shy young DC Ian Jenkins suddenly exclaimed.

"Ay?" Dewhurst frowned.

"The letter B was on Mrs Girding's kitchen calendar, wasn't it? We thought it stood for a person or place, and we couldn't work out what, could we? Well, perhaps she was having a delivery of shopping that afternoon from..."

"BestCo!" Denton exclaimed excitedly.

"Or Billock Mega Mart?" Jenkins proposed.

"They don't deliver," Karen Preece informed him. "They just about manage to serve you in the shop."

"It could well be what links the three women, given the presence of van tyre marks at Girding's house. Smart work, Jenkins," Dewhurst conceded grudgingly, feeling one of them should have spotted the rather obvious potential link a bit sooner, himself included.

The rather bashful young detective constable flushed bright red as Denton walloped him on the back.

"But there were no messages from any delivery drivers on either Lorraine Girding or Eve Beckford's land-lines or mobiles," Preece frowned.

"But there wouldn't be, if the delivery driver himself nabbed them, would there?" Denton replied.

Dewhurst raised a chubby hand in the air. "Hold your horses. Nobody's saying the local supermarket delivery driver has been kidnapping young – or not so young – mothers at home. What we're saying is that coincidentally, all three women could well use the same supermarket chain for their home delivery service. Perhaps someone, maybe an employee of BestCo, has gained illegal access to customer data to pinpoint targets."

"And then they turn up in a different van some time before, knowing their woman will be at home and ready to open the door to them?" Jenkins queried.

"Sounds pretty far-fetched to me," Denton grunted, pulling a face. "And why would a posh cow like Lorraine Girding use BestCo? Surely she'd use Sainsbury or E-topia?"

"They have far better delivery coverage," Preece informed him. "Lexington's a bit off the beaten track."

There was a brief pause as the team considered the possible method of abduction.

"You know, it does work," Preece said, finally.

Dewhurst stood up to his full height. "I need someone with tact and diplomacy to pay a visit to the Delivery Manager at BestCo."

"That rules you out, then, Dents," Preece grinned at Sean Denton.

"Karen – get in touch with the supermarket and arrange an appointment with them asap. We need access to their IT systems and operators. Take Quinn with you. Given the incident with Dave Sheffrey, I expect they'll guess it's in connection with our missing threesome, but be as discreet as possible."

"Yes, Sir."

"And Denton - liaise with Parlour. Run our ideas past him, see what he has to say, then organise a team to revisit the areas surrounding all three properties. I want you to ask again about any vans seen in the area. You might want to check out all the local petrol stations and ask for CCTV tapes for the days in question. A long shot and a horrible job for some poor sod in Technical Support, but there's every chance our van driver had to fill up if they were planning on taking the women on a journey."

Dewhurst paused briefly. "I don't need to remind you that we'll have the suits breathing down our neck, now that we've gone public. And the disappearance of DCI Parlour's missus will only increase the pressure. We're adding two and two together and hopefully making four, but we may be well off track – so keep an open mind. Are we all clear on what we're doing?"

There was a general grunt of affirmation followed by a shuffling of chairs.

25

Juliet woke up from her drug induced slumber some hours later to find herself lying on some mud flats. She lifted her head and was greeted with a wonderful view of a medieval castle across the estuary. Shivering, she drew her knees up to her chest and rose a shaky hand to her temple, which seemed to be sporting a large lump. It was a damp November afternoon, not the best time to find oneself dressed only in a cotton hoodie and jersey leisure pants. What had happened to her shoes? She closed her eyes and opened them again; no, she wasn't hallucinating. She really was sitting on a mud flat overlooking Portchester Castle.

Juliet pulled herself up shakily, exclaiming as she felt the mud ooze between her bare toes. She surveyed her surroundings; behind her in the distance was a blue building, some kind of leisure complex by the looks of it. And some posh apartments, beyond that. She hadn't been there for a good few years, but it looked like Port Solent. What on earth was she doing in Pompey, of all places?

Juliet raised a hand to her throbbing head as the full horror of what had happened back at Spatchcock Drive came back to her. But what was she doing here? Why had they dumped her out of the van? Why hadn't they taken her to the place where the Girding and Beckford women were being held hostage? Despite the inclement weather and the filthy state of her clothing, Juliet sensed she had somehow got off lightly.

She staggered back towards Port Solent. There was a tennis centre there, and a pub, as far as she could remember – she would be able to phone for help from there. *How dependent we've become on mobile phones,* Juliet thought to herself, watching where she put her bare feet, trying to avoid sharp stones or broken glass.

Fortunately, she did not have to suffer the indignity of walking into a public building caked in mud. A startled young lady placing a gym bag in the boot of her car saw Juliet approach her in the car park. Giving a brief explanation of what had happened to her, Juliet asked the girl to call the police on her behalf.

***

"I'm just glad I was driving around in the area," a mightily relieved Mark Parlour informed his wife later that evening, stroking her freshly washed and blow-dried blonde tresses as she lay in his arms in bed. "It was wonderful to get to you first... even if you did ruin my best Italian suit!"

"I'm glad too," Juliet murmured, burying her nose in her husband's skinny chest.

"Why didn't you call me first, though?" Parlour asked, still a little aggrieved that he had heard of his wife's re-appearance second-hand.

"I was filthy. My hands were all muddy – all I could think was, I'll ruin that poor girl's mobile. That's why I just got her to call 999."

"Silly Jules, I would have bought her a new mobile just to be first to hear your voice again." Parlour squeezed her tenderly and kissed her forehead.

"I know, I wasn't thinking. But you never know how you're going to react in such circumstances, do you?"

"I guess not," Parlour murmured. He fondled his wife's shapely bottom. What on earth had he been thinking of, finding the almost pre-pubescent figure of Karen Preece more attractive than the mature figure of his wife, the mother of his child? What was a bit of physical baggage when you considered what it represented. He thanked God silently that the brief dalliance with Preece had not gone too far and resolved to try harder to support his wife in this new sleep-deprived existence of theirs. At least Margaret and Derek had offered to hang onto Rowan overnight, a surprising and much

131

appreciated gesture from his rather peevish in-laws. This would enable Mark and Juliet to spend some precious time together alone, to recover from the horror of their ordeal and catch up on some much needed sleep.

"Promise me something, Jules?"

"What's that?" she murmured dozily.

"Promise me you'll never shop on-line again?"

Juliet chuckled into his chest. "That was my first and last foray into the world of internet grocery shopping!"

"I'm glad to hear it. But why did you keep it secret from me?"

Juliet shrugged. "Thought you would moan about the delivery charge. Kate D'Archeville suggested it, thought it would be less stressful for me than taking Ro shopping."

Hence the call to Jules's mobile instead of the landline, Parlour thought to himself. She was obviously calling for a discreet catch-up with Juliet. Poor Kate, Parlour thought to himself. She was only trying to help Jules and ended up sending her into the arms of the abductors and potential killers.

As his wife drifted off into a deep slumber, Parlour recapped on the events she'd outlined in her statement to Detective Superintendent Dewhurst and himself earlier that afternoon.

She'd just got showered and dressed when the doorbell rang at precisely 12 noon. Expecting BestCo and feeling pleased that they had turned up right at the start of the delivery window, thus enabling her to get on with her day, Juliet had rushed to the door. There she was confronted with a skinny lad with a shaven head and facial piercings, dressed in a navy checked shirt and slacks, as were all male employees of the popular supermarket. He had smiled, hands in pockets, and said *BestCo* before barging through the door. Wearing flesh coloured latex gloves, he had then brandished a small knife in Juliet's face just inside the porch, threatening to harm both Juliet and her baby if she didn't do as she was told. Terrified for her own life, but more for the life of baby Rowan, Juliet had complied with his instructions and followed him silently out of the house.

She had then been ordered to step into the back of a large white transit van which had been backed up in her driveway, feet away from her front door. Still bearing the knife, the shaven-headed man had then held a damp cloth smelling of chemicals over Juliet's nose and that was the last she could remember for a good half hour.

Some time later the effects of the chloroform had worn off and Juliet could make out snatches of a conversation in the front of the van. The skinny man was now sat in the passenger seat alongside the driver, and she found herself alone in the back of the transit van, lying on some kind of oily rag on the floor. She was surrounded by rolls of cable and various electrical items. For some reason, a wheelchair was folded up and stuffed under the shelving attached to one side of the van's interior. Through a mesh grill, she could make out the back of the two men's heads. The driver was beefy in build with a rippled red neck and a shaven head. Next to him sat the skinny man who had rung on her doorbell and threatened her at knifepoint. The skinny man sported a distinctive Beckhamesque tattoo which ran from his hairline down to the collar of his shirt. He was also shaven headed, his left ear riddled with stud earrings. She could also see a dog-eared A-Z of the Nord-Pas-de-Calais region of France, a snippet of information that could prove vital to the hitherto threadbare investigation.

They appeared to be having some kind of heated debate. Juliet struggled to make out much of what they were saying as the van rumbled along the road at high speed, but the word *cat* cropped up several times and there also seemed to be talk of a farm. Juliet could not supply any more information than that, though she could tell that the men were in a rather agitated state, as if a plan had been thwarted and they were forced to decide on an alternative course of action - which was precisely what had happened.

The skinny man made and received a number of calls on a mobile phone and shortly after that, they'd swerved over to the side of the road. They'd appeared to rejoin the main road before swinging off again. At that point, the skinny man had got out of the van, unlocked the back doors and thrown a startled Juliet down the bank towards the water. As she tumbled down the muddy slope, she had banged her head on a stone, which had knocked her cold again.

In her view, they had simply needed to ditch her asap; it hadn't been a pre-meditated attempt to drown her, and the tide was out in any case. The timing of events and the distance covered by the van suggested to Dewhurst and Parlour that Juliet had been abducted half an hour or so before the press release was aired on the local radio and television stations. On hearing that Parlour was still the SIO on the case at that point in time, the men had panicked and made a phone call to the ringleader of the gang. They had then clearly been advised to ditch the detective's missus, to Juliet's extreme good fortune, and had promptly done so just off the M275 at Port Solent.

All of which brought Dewhurst and Parlour to the rather obvious conclusion that the men were heading towards the international ferry port in Portsmouth. The wheelchair was to transport the drugged Juliet Parlour on board.

The innocuous white transit van, devoid of livery, but complete with workmen's tools and Sun newspaper on the dashboard, was nothing out of the ordinary. Such vans were a ubiquitous presence on the driveways of private residential streets all over the country and were a constant on the highways and byways of the nation.

As for the Calais A-Z:- in these days of European labour mobility, it was nothing to see a Hampshire registered van carrying out work on the continent. That said, Parlour felt it was far more likely that the street map had something to do with the abductions than an Anglo-French rewiring project. At a guess, the gang had obtained forged passports, which they had used to smuggle Lorraine Girding and Eve Beckford across the Channel.

Dewhurst had already requested CCTV footage and passenger records for all cross-Channel ferries leaving from Portsmouth for the period in question. Surely someone would remember a woman asleep (or rather droopy) in a wheelchair, accompanied either by two shaven-headed men or an accomplice of as yet unknown appearance. The chances of this were increased, if both Lorraine Girding and Eve Beckford had been taken across in this way. The white van with an H possibly 53 number plate must appear on CCTV at the port, too.

Meanwhile, there was the conundrum posed by the mention of cats and farms. The relevance of a farm was fairly obvious, as a potential holding place for the two abducted women, but what on earth did the farmyard cat have to do with anything?

Such thoughts occupied Parlour's brain as he closed his eyes and attempted to drift off to sleep.

26

"Who was that?" Grygor Jankowicz grumbled, as his wife returned from answering the telephone at 8am that morning and began to remove her nightwear.

"That idiot, Clump," Kat replied, spraying herself liberally with body spray. There was no time for a shower that morning; she'd have to Febreeze last night's clothes, too, for she hadn't had time to do the washing yet.

"But you're off today," Grygor frowned, sitting up in bed.

"I don't have to go in to *work* work, it's just a meeting. The police want to talk to some of us – I should be back in an hour or so."

"The police?"

"Don't sound so alarmed, I haven't been up to anything. Something to do with those women that went missing. Apparently, they all had their shopping delivered by us. The police want to talk to the internet shopping team, see if we can *assist with enquiries* as they always put it. I expect Aleks has had a call, too – she won't be too pleased; she was planning on getting started on her Christmas shopping today. "

"Can't say *I'm* best pleased," Grygor grumbled. "How will you get there, anyway? Cos I'm not getting out of bed to take you there!"

"Well, I know that! There's a bus just after 8.30. Better get a move on, though."

"So I need to deal with the kids? Great." Grygor slipped back under the duvet and rolled over on his side, back to his wife.

"For goodness sake, Grygor, it's a one off, and I have to deal with them the rest of the week. They're your kids too! Anyway, I shouldn't be long."

"You hope!" Grygor grunted.

"And you better not nod off again; they need to be out of here by twenty to nine."

Grygor just snorted and pulled the duvet up over his head.

***

Refreshed from the first decent night's sleep in about six months, it was with renewed vigour that DCI Mark Parlour bounced into Billock CID that Wednesday morning. Following a leisurely breakfast with his wife, followed by dessert in bed, Parlour had dropped Juliet off at her parents' house in Chave. Last night she had badly needed to recuperate from her ordeal and relax in her husband's arms, without jumping to the needs of baby Rowan. But that morning found Juliet desperate to hold her young son once more, her depth of feeling for him intensified by thoughts of what might have transpired.

Parlour was pleased to find both Dewhurst and Goodlove in the Incident Room on arrival at Billock Station. Goodlove had just returned from BestCo, whilst the pompous Dewhurst was revelling in his new capacity as SIO on the case.

Pleasantries were duly exchanged, with both men genuinely concerned for the welfare of Parlour's wife following her frightening journey into the unknown - which proved in the end to be no more than a muddy trip to Portsmouth.

"You'll appreciate, Parlour," Dewhurst began, once the three men sat down to business, "that though your missus has turned up, it would be preferable, all things considered, were I to remain SIO on this case."

Parlour nodded. "For once, Sir, I'm happy to hand over that responsibility to you. I'm determined to unmask these monsters, and not being SIO gives me far more freedom to fly with the prevailing wind, so to speak."

"Hmm," Dewhurst snorted, not too sure about Parlour's rather poetic turn of phrase but understanding the underlying

137

sentiment. "So, what have we learnt from Mrs P concerning our delightful wife-nappers?"

Parlour pulled out his Blackberry and accessed the relevant screen containing notes from his conversations with his wife the previous afternoon.

"Basically, as we ascertained yesterday, we're looking at a team of at least three - probably the driver and passenger in the white van plus a person directing them. There may well be, in addition, a fourth person guarding the two ladies, wherever they're being held – though we have strong reason to believe Lorraine Girding and Eve Beckford were taken by car ferry to the continent on the afternoon of their respective abductions. My wife spotted a Calais region A-Z on the front dash, and they were driving in the direction of the ferry terminal in Portsmouth before they unceremoniously dumped her at Port Solent."

"There was a wheelchair in the back of the van, which suggests the women were drugged or somehow made to sit in a wheelchair. That should jog someone's memory and would be far easier to spot on any CCTV footage. Jules didn't memorise the number plate on the van, but said it was a Hampshire number plate and that she thought it was a 53 plate, though it could have been 58. Obviously that still leaves a large number of white transit van registrations to trawl through, but it at least narrows it down somewhat."

"The police artist is going to work with Jules today on the appearance of the two men – we're hoping the rather distinctive spider web tattoo on the back of the thin man's neck will also provide a lead. We'll get his picture circulated around the local tattoo parlours as soon as Jules has met with the sketch lady."

"Has Mrs P remembered any more snatches of conversation?" Dewhurst frowned, taking notes.

Parlour shook his head. "She said it was very difficult to hear over the road noise. All she could make out was the word farm, and they appeared to yell out the word cat – as in feline friend – a few times. Maybe it's some kind of codeword."

At that point, Goodlove stuck his pencil in the air. "I have a lead on that, but finish first."

Dewhurst looked quizzically at him, but Goodlove felt it was important for Parlour to finish first, lest they skip over any detail that later proved vital to the investigation.

"She just said they appeared quite focussed at first, but then something seemed to aggravate them. The fat chap driving seemed to freak out about something then the skinny chap was making endless calls back and fore on the mobile. There was lots of shouting and then they suddenly swerved off the road.

They proceeded to have a heated debate but Jules couldn't hear any of it as lorries were zooming past them on the inside lane. They then accelerated back onto the hard shoulder before turning off again."

"At that point, the skinny man got out of the van, unlocked the back doors and chucked Jules down a muddy embankment. They then roared off again in the van. Jules thinks she banged her head as she fell which knocked her out cold again for a while – so unfortunately, she didn't see what direction they headed off in. My guess is, they turned back and ditched the van somewhere."

Dewhurst exhaled loudly. "So, we still have two missing women on our hands, but at least something to go on, at long last."

"I might have more for you, boss," Goodlove said eagerly, leaning forward across the table. He opened his pocketbook and cleared his throat.

"As you know, I arranged an early morning appointment with the delivery manager at BestCo on Billock West Industrial Estate – chap by the name of Paul Gregson. Karen couldn't get hold of him yesterday. Mr Gregson oversees the on-line grocery delivery service."

"They currently have a fleet of twelve vans, though that's due to increase, each working approximately within a twenty mile radius of Billock West BestCo. Areas beyond that are covered by Winchester, Portsmouth or Southampton East. Drivers either work an early, from 8am to 4pm or a late, from 4pm to midnight. There are twenty registered drivers currently, though figures do fluctuate. It's a fairly stressful job and consequently there's a pretty high turnover of staff. I interviewed fourteen of these 20 staff this morning. Karen interviewed Dave Sheffrey yesterday, so I left him out. Two of the others were on holiday and have been for the duration of the disappearances, and three were off sick today. I've arranged for all five to be interviewed at a location convenient to them."

"Of the fourteen I interviewed this morning, nobody had a bad word to say about our Mr Sheffrey and it was unanimously agreed that he wouldn't harm a fly, let alone abduct innocent women and keep them hostage. Though we will be checking through all fourteen's alibis, I found nothing suspicious on any of them. I questioned Gregson about who might have access to the on-line shopping orders and therefore the personal details of the ladies in question. I then interviewed the on-line order processors, a Mrs Rebecca Lunt and a Mr Tim Foss. Both denied passing on personal data to any third parties. I then queried how much of the information on the on-line grocery orders was made available to the personal shoppers, the staff who actually pick and bag the shopping in store for the customer. In the interests of privacy and data protection, only a customer reference number and the order itself appear on the consoles of the personal shoppers."

Parlour drummed his pen on the table, frowning. "Don't all BestCo computers have access codes? Their systems must be able to record anyone illegally accessing customer records – data protection and all that."

"I didn't consider that angle, boss," Goodlove conceded rather sheepishly, who wasn't as IT savvy as his senior colleague, or Karen Preece.

"So where's this leading?" Dewhurst interjected impatiently.

"Well, it seems to me that there are two explanations, if the link between the three women is indeed BestCo," Parlour replied, assuming control. "Firstly, someone is hacking into their computer system and printing off details of women at home. Or secondly, an employee is abusing the data protection laws and picking out women of a certain age and status. The function of these loyalty cards that most customers use, is that they provide a means by which the store can gather information about the customer's shopping habits – customer profiling. This information will be further modified by their postcode – i.e. are they thoroughly middle-class Yummy Mummies from Upper Chave or Benefit Cases from Billock? It will be fairly obvious, therefore, which customers are mothers of babies or small children by the regular purchase of nappies, or baby food, or chicken nuggets, etc. The postcode will give a good indication of what social class these mothers are – you get the picture."

"And they hazard a guess that the woman will be at home, on the basis that she's having her shopping delivered?" Dewhurst surmised.

Parlour nodded. "Indeed. They also know whether she is wealthy or not by the type of food on the bill. Delivery itself is not a sign of wealth – it's only four or five quid after all, which is not prohibitive for all but the hardest up in society – you easily make that money back by a combination of what you save on petrol, and by not being tempted by impulse buys. Though, admittedly, you'd need a degree of intelligence to have worked that out – a commodity which is obviously not exclusive to the middle classes, but..."

Goodlove grinned as Parlour dug himself a hole.

"So how do they pull this scam?" Dewhurst frowned, who was feeling rather slow on the uptake that day.

"Easy," Goodlove shrugged. "They know that the delivery has been booked for between 12 and 2, using Juliet's example. They then back the white van right up to the front door, probably bang on or just before the start of the delivery slot, and ring the doorbell. When the woman comes to the door, they urge her into the van at knifepoint."

"What if the woman doesn't answer the door?" Dewhurst enquired.

Goodlove shrugged again. "They drive off at speed, try another victim another day."

Parlour frowned. "What if she sees them and reports them?"

"They just say they're on a job and got the wrong house – they've got a white van stashed with electrical gear after all."

"But what if the real BestCo delivery truck turns up at the same time?" Parlour persisted.

"Again, they just drive off – who's going to think much of it? Reversing into the wrong driveway is hardly a criminal offence. And the type of clothes worn by BestCo drivers are easily obtained in the weekend casuals department of most chainstores – there's dozens of men out there mooching about in navy checked shirts and chinos and they don't all work for BestCo."

"It does explain why they don't hit on wealthier clients," Parlour nodded. "It would be far more difficult to pass through an intercom security device with a close circuit surveillance camera."

"Shame neither Girding nor Beckford have CCTV set up," Dewhurst mused. "You'd think Girding in particular would have – especially given how precious he is about his wife and kid."

Parlour nodded in agreement. "There is one problem with this theory, though."

"What then?" Dewhurst barked impatiently.

"If that's how the abductors did it, then surely the other two women must have had missed deliveries as well. Has anyone checked that out?"

"Not sure," Goodlove replied guiltily. In other words, no, Parlour thought.

"Maybe they just drove off," Dewhurst commented. "After all, not every driver's like Boy Wonder over at your place."

"Check it out, Cam," Parlour commanded.

"On it, boss."

"So, to cut it short, you think a BestCo employee is involved somewhere along the line?" Dewhurst surmised, drumming his pen on the table impatiently.

"Not necessarily," Parlour interjected. "It could be someone at Head Office or any branch where the customer database can be accessed. Though, I have to say, this would appear to be the work of someone with local knowledge."

Goodlove pulled a sheet of paper from his file. "I have here a list of all BestCo employees at Billock West. Amongst the one hundred and eight employees, there's a considerable Polish contingent. They work hard, apparently, and the majority have a pretty good grasp of English."

"And?" Dewhurst interrupted, wishing Goodlove would cut to the chase.

"Listed among the staff we have one Katerina Jankowiczowa, or..."

"Kat for short!" Dewhurst exclaimed, slapping the table with his hand.

"Exactly," Goodlove grinned. "We immediately thought of our four-legged friends, when Juliet told us the van drivers kept repeating the word *cat*. But they may well have been referring to a person by the name of Kat!"

"So have you brought her in for questioning yet, Goodlove?" Dewhurst demanded.

"Thought I'd better run the whole thing by you first, boss," Goodlove replied. "She was none too pleased at being dragged out of bed early on her day off, as it was. Thought I would make sure before we had a harassment case on our hands."

"What d'you think, eh, Parlour?" Dewhurst turned to his subordinate. "Reckon the theory fits?"

"It's a possibility, certainly," Parlour demurred. "Obviously money would be the motivating factor. But we need a lot more information before we start hurling accusations based on pure supposition..."

"But you admit it's worth following up, Parlour?" Dewhurst persevered, like a pack dog who'd picked up the scent after a long period in the olfactory wilderness.

"Well it's our only lead so far," Parlour conceded. "Though I'm not quite so sure we'd jump to the same conclusion if there was a Catherine Smith working at Billock BestCo. "

"But there isn't," Dewhurst interjected rather too hastily for Parlour's liking.

"Goodlove – bring Katerina Wotserface here for questioning, and..."

"Whoa!" Parlour interjected hastily. "It's just guesswork at the moment. We can't thunder in, all guns blazing. Cam's right - we'll have a racial harassment claim slapped on us before we know it. I think Cam should pay her a visit at home."

"Ok ok," Dewhurst backed down, holding his palms up in mock surrender. "What about her mates – any friends we should be interviewing, too?"

"She seemed bezzies with the woman sat next to her this morning." Goodlove consulted his list, recalling in his mind's eye in what sequence he had noted their names. "Bird with dyeded dark hair and glasses... got her. Aleksandra Kowalewa, also a Polish migrant worker."

"Interview her as well," Dewhurst commanded. "On second thoughts, you interview her, Parlour – preferably at the same time, so they can't come up with an alibi. Wait till Goodlove's already through the door at this Kat woman's place, then give Aleksandra a quick call to check she's in and nip round there pronto."

And I'll just go and suck eggs at the same time, Parlour thought to himself. Was he that patronising to his own junior staff, telling them how to do their job and stating the obvious at all times?

"We perhaps ought to check with Interpol and the Polish police, too," Parlour stated dryly, giving Dewhurst a hard stare before leaving the room.

27

Nice house, Parlour thought to himself, pulling up outside a large red brick newish build in Chave, just a few streets away from his in-laws' place. He'd been told, in his brief telephone conversation with a clearly annoyed Aleksandra Kowalewa, that the Kowals occupied an annexe to the rear of the property. Once a two storey garage, the Perkisses, who owned the property, had converted the rather over-the-top car storage area into a two up, two down dwelling. They were not the first on the development to do so, and surely wouldn't be the last. Commanding a rent of around a thousand a month, the loss of a double garage was a small sacrifice to make in the interests of paying off the mortgage early. A separate brick construction to the far left side of the property suggested the Perkisses had not struggled to gain planning permission for an alternative vehicular storage solution.

Parlour walked slowly to the front door of the garage conversion, his feet crackling loudly on the beige gravel. Aware that she was probably looking out for him, Parlour tried not to appear too fired up – it wouldn't do to create an atmosphere of tension before he had even struck up a conversation with Aleksandra Kowalewa. His suspicion that she had been watching out for him, was confirmed when she immediately opened the front door to him.

"Mrs Kowalewa?" Parlour enquired with impeccable pronunciation, having done his research first. "Detective Chief Inspector Mark Parlour, Billock CID. We spoke on the phone earlier."

Aleks looked behind him.

"I've come alone," Parlour smiled, sensing she'd been expecting extra officers and perhaps even a squad car. That was an interesting reaction in itself.

"May I?" Parlour enquired, indicating with his hand that she should ask him in.

"Of course, sorry," Aleks stuttered, embarrassed at her reaction to this smartly dressed and polished detective. "Come through. I've put some coffee on. The real stuff, not that horrible stuff in a jar you Brits still suffer."

"Not me," Parlour grinned. "I ditched the war rations years ago."

Aleks smiled, wondering whether the war reference was a deliberate attempt to put her at ease.

They made small talk about the weather and the Christmas shopping onslaught before taking seats opposite one another in a small but tastefully furnished living room.

"I understand you rent this house from a Mr A Perkiss?" Parlour enquired, opening his pocketbook and referring to Goodlove's notes from that morning.

"Yes, Tony owns a factory on Chave Park Industrial Estate – Perkiss Engineering - his own firm, of course. His wife, Kezia, is a Director, but in name only. She seems to be at home most of the time, lunching with ladies and such like."

Parlour grinned. "Your English is very good."

"Thank you," Aleks smiled. "I go to advanced evening classes at Billock College. I don't want to be one of those who come over and make no effort to fit in. I didn't just come over here to survive; I want to achieve."

"I can see you mean that," Parlour smiled, noting the M&S tailored surroundings. "Quite a cushy number for you, living here, isn't it?"

Kowalewa shrugged, not entirely sure how to take the smooth-talking DCI with his polished shoes and slicked back hair.

"Jan's a skilled worker. He landed the job with Mr Perkiss, who was looking for a hard-working, well-qualified machinery engineer. Tony – Mr Perkiss – was keen to keep hold of Jan and offered us this house to live in. It's a little strange living in the boss's garden, but the rent is very reasonable and it's better than getting stuck in some awful council owned high-rise in Billock."

"Like your mate, Kat?" Parlour enquired smoothly, raising his eyebrows.

"It's not Kat's fault," Aleks replied rather defensively, though not so fiercely that Parlour sensed she wouldn't speak against her friend under pressure.

"Her husband has a crappy job that pays peanuts and BestCo offers little more than pocket money – a bit extra to pay for the kids' clubs and swimming lessons and all the other middle-class rubbish that you're expected to enrol your kids in here."

"She must be a bit envious of you, then," Parlour noted nonchalantly. "You've got yourself well set up here, haven't you?"

Aleks shrugged. "Jan worked hard back at home to get qualified. He deserves everything he's got for us. Kat is a nice girl but she married a ..."

"Loser?" Parlour proposed, raising his eyebrows again.

"She didn't marry a career minded man," Aleks qualified herself. "He hasn't found it as easy to adapt to life in England."

"Do you ever sense that Kat feels angry with you – for what you've achieved over here?"

"Why are you so interested in Katerina?" Kowalewa frowned, peering at Parlour's notepad and trying to read it upside down. Parlour gently closed it and returned it to his inside pocket.

"Could you just answer the question?" Parlour persisted.

Kowalewa stood up, draining the coffee from her cup and banging it down on the tray. "Look – I understand you need to question the staff, but I don't know why you are homing in on me and Kat. Just because we are not English doesn't mean you can barge into our homes and accuse us of being involved in these kidnappings! Why would either of us be interested in abducting these women? We are both mothers, we know the hell these ladies must be going through – we are decent women who respect the law. Why would we want to do such a thing?”

"For the money?" Parlour suggested.

Kowalewa laughed hollowly and gestured around the room. "Clearly I am living on the breadline," she stated sarcastically.

"And your friend?"

Kowalewa took a deep breath. "Look, Mr Parlour, I have nothing to do with this horrible business. And I can't imagine Katerina has, either. Just because these women used our supermarket, I don't see that it gives you lot the right to interrogate and cast suspicion on the staff!"

"But you already stated that Katerina Jankowiczowa is short of money. "

"Short of money, yes. Jealous that I've landed on my feet, as you put it, I think so, yes. But dishonest – never in a million years."

"Would you swear by that in court?" Parlour asked smoothly.

"If need be," Kowalewa replied uncertainly. The manner of her response was duly noted.

As Parlour left the house, he noted that Kowalewa seemed to be aware that Katerina Jankowiczowa was also receiving a police visit at that time. They had not informed her of the fact; clearly Jankowiczowa had seized an opportune moment to send a quick text to her friend prior to his arrival. That could be viewed as suspicious, and Parlour made a mental note to request a record of Jankowiczowa's mobile phone calls and texts that morning.

28

"So how was Mrs Jankowiczowa?" Parlour enquired of DS Goodlove, over a pot of tea in the conservatory back at Spatchcock Drive. Normality had been restored at home following a brief period as a crime scene.

Parlour had understandably not wanted to leave his wife alone for too long following the previous day's events. He had insisted that she ring him the moment she returned from her parents' house in Chave, baby Rowan in tow. The police sketch artist was due in a little while.

"Defensive and not entirely convincing, if you want the honest answer, guv," Goodlove replied.

"Oh? In what way?"

"Well, she seems to operate on three settings, does our Kat. Sleep, work, watch telly."

"As do the vast majority of working-class people with kids, Cam," Parlour stated.

"Possibly," Goodlove replied. "But she was immediately sure when questioned that she had been watching television on the evenings following the first two abductions. Said that her husband was with her on both occasions, and he backed her statement up. She was working on all three mornings in question."

"Well, we know that's true – that she was working those mornings," Parlour stated. "And what else are you supposed to do of a weekday evening, if you've young kids at home and no spare cash?"

"It was just the way she immediately jumped down my throat and said they'd been watching telly, before I'd even given her the dates. As if she was nervous and had prepared a response."

"I should imagine if you're a migrant worker and a senior police officer comes knocking on your door, you would be nervous, Cam. Put yourself in her shoes."

"I don't think I could quite manage that, Guv," Goodlove grinned, looking down at his size 13 feet. "But point taken."

"Sorry, not trying to pour cold water over your theory, it just sounds like she was nervous. You are pretty larger than life, you know! Even if we all know you're a complete pussy... and that's not a homophobic comment, before you go all Lin Dawe on me!"

"No offence taken. And I hear what you're saying, Sir, but she still seemed twitchy all the same."

"Maybe her husband is up to no good and she thought we'd got wind of that."

"Is that a racist assumption, Sir?" Goodlove grinned.

Parlour shook his head. "It's a realistic stab at why the wife of a low-earning working-class man in Billock Towers should be rather furtive when the police come knocking."

"Or they're up to their necks in the abductions and conveniently live in a flat overlooking the ransom handover point," Goodlove counter-punched.

"There's that, obviously," Parlour concurred. "I just don't think we should leap to conclusions. I've not come across many working-class people in all my years in the Police Service who don't come over all defensive when the police come knocking!"

"Why don't you interview her then, and see what you think?" Goodlove said, not intending to sound sulky but managing it nonetheless.

"Maybe I'll have to," Parlour replied a touch mysteriously.

"Oh?"

"As you know, I paid a visit to her best mate Aleks this morning. Her husband wasn't there. She lives in a smart little garage conversion in the back garden of a Mr Tony Perkiss's property."

"Perkiss? As in the engineering company on the industrial estate near your outlaws? I think I drove past it last week when I paid a visit to that dodgy tyre plant."

"That's the one," Parlour nodded. "Her husband works for Perkiss. He's pretty handy under the bonnet and Perkiss was keen not to lose a man with his mechanical skills – you know what kids are like these days. Very few are actually skilled in anything of practical use – they all want to be prancing around miming to a backing track. Those who can actually do something useful milk it for all it's worth and call the shots. Perkiss was so keen to keep Jan Kowal on, he offered his family his new garage conversion for rent. Kowal is obviously earning a fair amount, because the house was immaculate inside. M&S leather sofas and chunky oak furniture. Not a faux-leather CD cabinet in sight."

"Pleased to hear it," Goodlove shuddered, who did conform to stereotype when it came to home interiors.

"Aleks told me that Kat was an honest and upstanding citizen and wouldn't dream of being involved in such a scheme."

"As she would," Goodlove interjected.

"I felt she was genuine," Parlour said slowly, choosing his words carefully. "But I did get the impression that..."

"What?"

"I got the impression that Kat was jealous of Aleks and the house."

"Understandable," Goodlove nodded, his heart quickening.

"It wouldn't surprise me if Kat feels distinctly hard done by."

"Enough to arrange for three women to be kidnapped?" Goodlove wondered.

"We have a financial motive, and we have a means – assuming Kat or an acquaintance has the know-how to access customer details."

"What about the ransom handover point, as well, Sir?" Goodlove began excitedly. "In the wasteland beyond Billock Towers! They could probably nip down in the advert break of *Corrie* and pick up the ransom."

Parlour frowned. "I'm not sure about that – you'd think if Katerina Jankowiczowa was involved, she'd try and point the finger away from her and keep the action well away from her own backyard."

"But if she had a jumbo chip on her shoulder about rich bitches, then she'd want to make them see things from her perspective. This is how it is for the other half. Hence the value cereal box thing, too! *Welcome to my world, ladies!"*

"It does all fit, Cam, I grant you that."

Goodlove was gathering momentum now. "I really do think we're onto something, boss! It's pretty obvious to me that she's the "cat" Juliet overheard hem talking about in the van! What are we waiting for? Let's get her up here asap to answer some questions!"

Parlour held his hand up. "Hold it right there! It's pure supposition. We have to be very careful when it comes to migrant workers. I need to have a word with the Super first."

And DI Preece, Parlour thought privately, whose intuition he rated far higher than the Superintendent's.

***

Parlour also ran the theory past his wife, who was now fully party to the investigative process, having played a leading role in the drama unfolding. Juliet had conceded that the hypothesis made sense, but – interestingly – felt that it somehow rang untrue. At that precise moment in time, she couldn't for the life of her think why.

One interesting point emerged from their discussion, however. In touching on the subject of Polish migrant workers, Juliet suddenly recalled, a mite shamefully, the complaint she had lodged with the Store Manager of BestCo regarding two members of staff smoking outside the foyer the other week.

"They seemed Eastern European, though I couldn't say if they were Polish or not," Juliet frowned.

"In what way?" Parlour quizzed her.

"The language they were speaking sounded Eastern European... and they looked it. You know, naturally really pretty but with too much make up. One of them had that awful purple henna stuff in her hair."

Katerina Jankowiczowa had that coloured stuff in her hair, Parlour thought to himself. So did Aleksandra Kowalewa, for that matter, though hers was less obvious and looked like it had been done at a salon, not over the bathroom sink with some plastic gloves and a length of cling-film.

"It was a bit of an arsey way to behave, thinking about it now," Juliet conceded. "I was in a bad mood and they were just standing there gossiping, puffing smoke rings in the air like there was no tomorrow."

"Less tomorrows than us, that's for sure," Parlour said grimly, who detested the habit. He resented the way that innocent people were denied access to hospital beds and other vital NHS resources, whilst those who had contributed to their own respiratory downfall, seemed to qualify immediately for expensive cancer treatments and palliative care. Parlour was not a racist – this was not about non-British nationals accessing the Health Service, but it was very much about the irresponsible usurping the place of the blameless.

"It was a bit *Inspector Calls* of me, though," Juliet continued guiltily. "You know, where the daughter gets the shop girl sacked. I hope I didn't cause anyone to lose their job; that was never my intention."

"I wouldn't worry, Jules," Parlour smiled fondly at her, brain ticking over, evaluating the information she had just imparted to him. "You won't be the first hoity-toity middle-class housewife to flex some hormonal muscle in a supermarket, and you certainly won't be the last – though

admittedly Utopia is the main forum for it round these parts.
And smoking *is* a filthy habit; you're right."

29

Much to Detective Superintendent Christopher Dewhurst's frustration, the Ports Authorities came back with no suspicious sightings of wheel-chaired women boarding any cross-channel ferries from Portsmouth for the period in question. It was the same story at all the other southern ports and at the Channel Tunnel terminal in Folkestone. It was a tad premature, therefore, to start scouring the Pas-de-Calais for abandoned farm outhouses. Shame, Dewhurst thought to himself. He could do with a cross-channel jolly to replenish the old drinks cabinet. He'd heard there was a thumping great Carrefour in that Cité Europe place just a few roundabouts away from the French end of the tunnel. Apparently it even had a BestCo wine store there, too. The unsophisticated Dewhurst was not one to turn his bulbous nose up at globalisation; it made the world a more familiar place to him.

Thwarted at every turn, Dewhurst therefore had no hesitation in arranging for Katerina Jankowiczowa to be brought in for questioning; a failed line of enquiry was better in terms of placating the whips, than no lines of enquiry at all. It was easier to get her in for questioning than attempt to search her flat at this juncture. Dewhurst knew he would not be granted a search warrant for her flat on pure supposition – however snugly the pieces fitted.

"I don't feel right about this," Parlour conceded to Karen Preece that morning, as Dewhurst ordered a squad car be sent round to Billock Towers to pick up Jankowiczowa. "It's just a little too convenient, if you know what I mean."

Preece nodded. "But I don't see what alternatives we have at present. After all, we're not arresting her or anything, we are genuinely asking her to assist in our enquiries – to rule her in or out."

"Hopefully the early start will throw the local press," Parlour stated without conviction, himself rather thrown by Dewhurst's decision to haul them all in at 7am that morning. Parlour had to admit, it was prudent in the circumstances; the local and national press had been sniffing around Billock Station as soon as the press release concerning the missing ladies had been broadcast.

"So who's in the room with her?"

"Goodlove and yourself. The Super wants to watch with me outside. She's requested a Polish interpreter in case she doesn't understand everything we're asking – we've got hold of the Police contracted one - and her mate Aleks has given her the name of a local solicitor."

Preece raised her eyebrows. "Bit OTT, isn't it? Something to hide? Do we know the solicitor? Not a partner of our friend Mr Girding, I assume?"

"A James Patterson from Robes and Forster."

"Never heard of him," Preece stated, shaking her head.

"A pal of Mr Perkiss, I believe. Perkiss is paying."

Preece made a face. "A tad generous, wouldn't you say? Not only does he provide migrant accommodation in his back garden, he now supplies legal aid to friends of his tenants. Rather odd, wouldn't you say, boss?"

Parlour grinned. "There *are* some decent people left in the world, you know Karen."

Preece snorted. "There's always a motive, trust me. And if not exactly a motive, some internal craving for approval or favour."

"Cynic!" Parlour chuckled.

***

A visibly nervous Katerina Jankowiczowa was brought into the sole interview room at Billock Station at around 8.20 am

157

that Thursday morning. She took a seat beside her solicitor, with the Polish interpreter sat discreetly behind, ready to step in if called upon.

Karen Preece took a seat opposite, to the left of Cameron Goodlove, who was to lead the questioning. Watching the other side of the tinted glass were Dewhurst and Parlour.

Goodlove started the tape running. "The time is 8.21 am on Thursday 17 November 2011. Present in the interview room are Katerina Jankowiczowa, Mr James Patterson, her solicitor and Mrs Olga Malinowska, a Polish interpreter. Interviewing are Detective Sergeant Cameron Goodlove and Detective Inspector Karen Preece, both of Billock CID."

Before Goodlove could begin his questioning, a shaking Jankowiczowa enquired whether she was being arrested.

"At this moment in time, we simply want to eliminate you from our enquiries," Goodlove replied.

"Is this not a rather heavy-handed approach if you are merely seeking to rule Mrs Jankowiczowa out of abducting these women, as you will inevitably have to?" James Patterson enquired, peering at Goodlove from behind ridiculous half frame purple spectacles. "It all seems rather over the top, recording my client as well!"

As bent as a ha'penny piece, Goodlove thought, who prided himself on his macho appearance for a gay man, and only rarely paid homage to the queen inside. One of these rare occasions had been on national television, however.

"Possibly," Preece conceded, "but it was Mrs Jankowiczowa's choice to involve a solicitor and an interpreter."

"Can you tell me where you were on each of the following evenings?"

Preece proceeded to list a number of dates from the previous ten days.

"I've already told you," Jankowiczowa replied in thickly accented but entirely comprehensible English. "I spend the evenings at home watching television with my husband Grygor. We never go out."

"Every evening?" Preece frowned. "Can anyone vouch for that, besides your husband?"

"We didn't invite the neighbours in to join us, if that's what you mean," Jankowiczowa replied sarcastically. "Look, we have two children and no family to babysit. We waved goodbye to a social life when we moved to England."

Preece shuffled her sheets of A4 paper. "We've traced a number of calls from your mobile phone to Aleksandra Kowalewa's last week, plus a text to Kowalewa's phone shortly before my boss visited her this morning."

Jankowiczowa shrugged. "She's my best friend over here; I expect I called her to arrange a lift to work or something. And yes I did text her this morning - not because I have anything to hide. I just thought she would want to know that I was being pestered by you guys. She would want to know."

She looked mutinously at Preece and Goodlove.

"Do you normally travel to work together?" Goodlove enquired, who was most definitely not a morning person, and couldn't imagine anything worse than attempting to make conversation with someone first thing in the morning on a regular basis.

"Sometimes we get the bus, sometimes her husband takes us straight from school – if we're running late or something. But we don't always start at the same time. So I often get a bus alone – there's one that leaves from near the school just after nine."

"Do you enjoy your job, Mrs Jankowiczowa?" Goodlove asked.

Again that non-committal shrug. "It's money, isn't it? It helps with the bills and the people are ok – mostly."

"Could you clarify mostly?"

"We get some rude customers but my colleagues are all very friendly. We all get on well, there's a nice... how do you say it?"

"Atmosphere?" Preece suggested.

Jankowiczowa nodded. "Yes, a nice atmosphere."

"But some of the customers are rude?" Goodlove prompted her, following a verbal nudge in his earpiece from Parlour.

Jankowiczowa shrugged once more. "We get some very cross..." she struggled for the phrase, "OAPs."

"Are they the worst?" Goodlove prodded.

"No... the stuck up ones are the worst, those women from the suburbs, and that poxy designer town, Devington, or whatever it's called."

Preece suppressed a grin, aware of Parlour watching through the tinted glass.

"In what way are they rude?" Goodlove enquired.

James Patterson began blustering about the seemingly digressive nature of the DI's questioning but was promptly put in his place by a sharp-tongued Karen Preece.

"They treat us like slave labour," Jankowiczowa replied disdainfully, as if to mimic their condescension. "Can you fetch this, can you fetch that, can you get me a trolley with wheels that point in the same direction, can't you find a job back home – that sort of thing."

The anger in her tone was palpable. James Patterson shot Jankowiczowa a baleful look, imploring her to stop digging a hole for herself.

Goodlove felt his heart race, sensing his instincts were right.

"So you've faced racist comments from these lady customers. Can you remember on how many occasions?"

Jankowiczowa shook her head. "Many times. They don't say it directly perhaps, but they mean it that way. They make comments about how many of us Poles work in the shop. They don't make comments about how many English women work there – or Asians, for that matter. They speak to us differently."

"How do they speak differently to you?" Goodlove probed.

"They're not so polite," Jankowiczowa replied. "As if they are talking to children – very deaf, stupid children. We're not meant to fetch and carry for the customers. We're busy with our internet shopping orders. They see us walking up and down the aisles with our trolleys and they think we are available to do work for them. It is not the case."

"What happens if you refuse to help them?"

Jankowiczowa made a neck slitting gesture with her left hand which Goodlove explained for the tape.

"I get my manager, Mr Clump, after me, if I am late doing an order."

"And how do these middle-class women react – if you refuse to interrupt your work to help them?"

"Sometimes they're rude; sometimes they even complain to the Manager about me."

"Do you know the names of any women who have done so?" Goodlove asked, as Parlour prompted him once more on the earpiece.

Jankowiczowa shook her head. "I don't know. We're not told their names; we are just told that a customer has complained about this or that and then we're told to do better or we'll lose our jobs."

Preece wondered what employment rights these women had, who had maybe only recently entered the workforce in this country. Surely a supermarket group the size of BestCo would adhere fairly stringently to employment law, though?

"How do you feel when these women complain?" Goodlove asked.

"I feel angry, I feel hurt, but I forgive them eventually," Jankowiczowa replied.

"You do feel angry, though?" Goodlove checked.

"I feel anger, yes. But I am a Christian lady, Detective Sergeant. I forgive them. I know they are just stupid, and ignorant, and know nothing of real life. They wouldn't be like that if they lived my life. So I have to forgive them."

"You say you are a Christian," Goodlove enquired smoothly. "Do you attend a local church, Mrs Jankowiczowa?"

"What relevance, if any, do Mrs Jankowiczowa's religious beliefs have on this investigation?" Patterson objected.

"We are investigating the abduction of three wives and mothers, Mr Patterson," Preece replied icily. "I would say Mrs Jankowiczowa's views on the sanctity of human life and Christian family values are highly relevant – wouldn't you?"

"You can value human life without being a church-goer," Patterson retorted, eyeing Goodlove and willing him to agree.

"I am a good Catholic girl. There is an orthodox Polish Catholic church in Billock, but it's not always possible for me to go," Jankowiczowa stated.

"Why not?" Goodlove asked.

"I have to work every other Sunday. I don't want to, but I have to."

"Why don't you want to?" Goodlove probed.

"Because it is not right to work on Sundays. But you don't care in this country – I saw you all nosing around our tower block at the weekend. Don't you have families to care for?"

"This is a potential murder enquiry, Mrs Jankowiczowa," Goodlove reminded her dryly.

"All people do here is work work work, and when you're not working, you are shopping. You're always buying things to keep up with everyone else. If you didn't buy so much, you wouldn't have to work such crazy hours and you wouldn't feel this pressure. You would have more of a life. People back home in Poland don't have all this stuff that you have over here."

How very true, Preece thought to herself.

"What sort of stuff?" Goodlove pressed, ignoring another protest from Patterson.

Jankowiczowa shrugged, unaware of where this was heading. "Furniture, designer clothes, and all these pointless electronic things like Wii fit that everyone thinks they must have."

"Do you have electronic things at home?"

"Some things, yes," Jankowiczowa frowned. "But we have to save all the time and find a bargain. Who's going to give us one of your endless credit cards?"

"Do you own a home computer, Mrs Jankowiczowa?" Goodlove persevered.

"My husband has a laptop. But it's very old. We do not have an internet connection. He plays games on it, that's all."

"So you don't use it?"

Jankowiczowa spread her hands out. "No! It would be nice to send emails to my family at home or to use one of those web camera things, but we cannot afford all that satellite television and broadband stuff."

"Do you have access to a computer at work?"

Jankowiczowa shook her head. "No. I have the computer screen on my trolley, that's all."

"Are there any customer details on your console – names, addresses, for example?"

Jankowiczowa shook her head again. "Just an order number."

"So you have no way of accessing personal details of customers?"

"No."

"Do you know anyone who might be able to access such details?" Goodlove enquired.

Jankowiczowa shook her head, suddenly looking bewildered. The expression of bewilderment was soon followed by one of angry enlightenment. "You think I found out where those women lived, don't you?"

She unleashed a torrent of Polish vitriol.

"Mrs Jankowiczowa expressed extreme displeasure that you should suspect a good Catholic woman such as herself of such evil deeds, and ... um... cast suspicion on the Sergeant's relationship to his mother," Olga Malinowska obliged.

Preece grinned. "I thought good Catholic girls didn't come out with such expressions."

"I'm sorry – I was angry," Jankowiczowa apologised. She looked down at her fingers and subconsciously rubbed her gold wedding band, before looking up at Goodlove.

"I have no way of finding out customer details. And I would never do such a thing. I don't like these ladies when they talk down at me, but I would never do anything to harm them. I wouldn't seek revenge on them."

"Detective Sergeant Goodlove, may I enquire on what basis you have judged it vaguely appropriate to bring my client here at this unsociable hour, at considerable inconvenience to herself and her family, simply to put a few questions to her? And why you have felt the need to record this interview?"

"The third lady to be abducted, a Mrs Juliet Parlour, was thrown from a vehicle," Goodlove replied, playing his trump card. "We have therefore been able to interview her about her kidnappers. She stated that she had quite clearly heard the two men who abducted her use the word cat or refer to a person by the name of Kat."

"Perhaps they were wondering who would feed the cat while they were out?" Jankowiczowa shrugged sarcastically. "Why do you assume it's me?"

"She also heard them talk about a farm. Does that mean anything to you?"

"No."

Goodlove drummed his pencil impatiently on the desk. This was not going quite as he intended; Kat Jankowiczowa could neither be ruled in or out on the basis of this interview. For an innocent woman, she was incredibly jumpy. And for one so religious, she had a foul mouth on her, too.

30

Parlour felt confused as he returned to his office. In his gut, he did not feel that Kat Jankowiczowa was involved in the abductions. Yet it couldn't be denied that she had not done herself any favours in the taped interview. Edgy and defensive, she had painted a picture of a woman battling away to make ends meet in an alien culture. It would be entirely understandable that she should feel envious, even bitter towards the likes of Eve Beckford and Lorraine Girding. They were women who must seem to Kat to have it all on a plate - the rich husband, the smart house, the time to enjoy their family of a weekend - none of the endless scrimping and saving just to put food on the table and electricity in the meter.

Dewhurst wanted to search her flat. Both of them knew they would be unlikely to be granted a search warrant in the circumstances, given the lack of evidence against Jankowiczowa and the plenitude of pure supposition. Parlour wasn't sure what was to be gained by a house search – if Kat did hold information on the missing ladies, she would be unlikely to be daft enough to leave it lying around the flat, now that she had been interviewed at the station. Now that they'd shown their hand, it was unlikely CID would find anything of use there, full stop.

All the same, it would be interesting to double-check the view from the fifteenth floor over Fryer's Dip and suss out the neighbours. And if Kat was as innocent as she made out, then she shouldn't object to a police search; they might yet turn up something of relevance to the investigation.

Parlour picked up the phone. "Denton? Can you pay a visit to the Polish Orthodox church in Billock. Find out if Kat Jankowiczowa is a regular member of the congregation. Thanks."

He sifted through the recently arrived internal mail and checked his phone messages and emails. There was still no further information on the whereabouts of the two missing women. Parlour gritted his teeth; he knew that the longer they remained missing, the less likely they were to be found alive.

There was a knock on the door; it was Karen Preece.

"Boss – I've just put the phone down to Robert Girding. I was just bringing him up to speed with events, thought it was only fair."

Parlour nodded. "And?"

"And, he revealed that his wife had been battling depression for some time. He didn't want to mention it earlier; said she's been off the happy pills for a good year or so and didn't feel it was relevant. He felt, perhaps understandably, that if he mentioned it, we might not treat her abduction as seriously. But now she's been missing for so long, I guess he's worried about her state of mind."

"Mmm," Parlour nodded, thinking briefly of his own wife's rather teary demeanour of late and uttered an internal prayer of gratitude for her safe, if somewhat fortuitous, escape from the clutches of the kidnappers. "Thanks for telling me, Karen. It certainly adds impetus to the need to find these women asap. I'll pass the info on to Dewhurst."

Preece nodded and left the office, as Olga Malinowska knocked on Parlour's open door. Parlour got up and shook the attractive Polish woman's hand. Unlike the rather downtrodden Katerina Jankowiczowa, Malinowska was someone who made the very most of herself. Today she was classically dressed in a black cashmere sweater and suede skirt, with a boldly patterned red silk scarf draped loosely around her long neck. With lustrous blonde hair resting on narrow shoulders, she was as sartorially sumptuous as Jankowiczowa was chainstore cheap.

"Detective Inspector Parlour, may I entreat you away from your desk for a coffee?"

"Do you have anywhere in mind?" Parlour grinned, who had worked with Malinowska on a previous case involving a Polish builder falsely accused of the theft of several hundred thousand pounds worth of modern art from a gallery in Foxburgh. "Because you wouldn't want to wash your dishes in the stuff they serve downstairs!"

"You took me to a little deli around the corner from here the last time we had the pleasure of working together," Malinowska smiled playfully, with the benign charm of a serial flirt. "Will it be open this early?"

"There's only one way to find out," Parlour smiled, grabbing his coat. He could afford to go AWOL for an hour or so; it had been an early start and he was no longer SIO on the case. In any case, he could gain some valuable background information on the Polish mindset from Malinowska which could prove more than a little relevant to the case.

Within ten minutes, Parlour was sipping an Americano, eagerly anticipating a slice of Gianni's best Sicilian orange cake.

"For what it's worth, I do not think Katerina is your man, so to speak," Malinowska stated, plopping four sugar cubes into her cappuccino. Parlour, who liked his coffee black and bitter, winced.

"What makes you say that, then?" Parlour enquired, choosing not to play his hand at this juncture.

Malinowska shook her head slowly, stirring the sugar into her coffee with a clockwise motion, followed by an anti-clockwise action of equal duration, a measured and calculated action that spoke of a methodical temperament.

"It's just not very... *Polish.*"

"What isn't?"

"Jealousy. Anger. Bitterness. Revenge. Polish people are, by and large, honest, hard-working types. They come over here to earn money to support their families. Much of industrial Poland is grey and depressing; they come here in search of the better life."

Billock Towers? Parlour thought to himself, picturing the grotty wasteland full of upturned shopping trolleys and dirty plastic bags, where the kidnappers had demanded the ransoms be left.

"They don't come to make trouble, as a rule," Malinowska continued. "And many of the women are good Catholics at heart, even these days."

"I'm having that checked out as you speak," Parlour informed her, accepting with gratitude his slice of cake from an unshaven but nevertheless obscenely good-looking Italian student, who had probably been dragged out of an upstairs bedsit by the boss when they'd arrived soon after opening time.

"She may not go to Mass regularly, but you'll probably find that she's retained a core of decency."

"But how do you quantify that?" Parlour wondered, mouth full of orange cake.

Malinowska shrugged. "It's a gut feeling, I suppose. I'm no criminal psychologist, but she just did not seem the type to be involved in a kidnapping ring, that's all."

"So who do you think is behind this?"

"I think this is a British class thing," Malinowska replied crisply, with the confidence of one who is sure of their ground. "This is someone who is madly, insanely jealous of these women, with their well-off husbands and their big, posh houses. She – because I think it is a woman behind this – wants to really make these women suffer. She wants them to see what life is like for her – hence the placing of the ransom money in a value cereal box, in some wasteland behind an ugly council housing development. I do not think it is her intention to kill them, because that would get at the husband, not the wife, if that is any comfort to you. It is more about slow torture – separating these women from their children, their doting husbands, their cushy lives. And, what is more, I think this woman has experienced a better life but has fallen on hard times. This is a woman who is aware of class divisions, which often demonstrate themselves in diet and product selection."

"And I thought you were just an interpreter," Parlour grinned, though he had already arrived at some of her conclusions himself.

"You don't need a degree in Criminal Profiling to work it out – perhaps just an outsider's perspective," Malinowska shrugged.

"Actually, I had reached much the same conclusion, I just wanted to see what you thought without prejudice," Parlour smiled, not wishing to lose face.

"But Dewhurst still wants to search her flat."

"She would be stupid to refuse," Malinowska stated. "Though she probably has every right. I would not fight with your DS Dewhurst!"

"He's a bit of a beast, isn't he?" Parlour grinned. "They call him Super Sausage back at the station. You've heard of Dewhurst the Butchers?"

Malinowska nodded, having been resident in the country for some ten years now and an ardent anglophile for considerably longer. "And I gather you are referred to as The Pizza?"

"You're not supposed to know that," Parlour smiled, rather embarrassed, passing a hand lightly over his acned cheek.

"The Mediterranean is good for a complexion such as yours, I hear," Malinowska stated, green eyes crinkled up at the corners. "How about a retirement villa in Italy?"

"Whoa! Retirement's a while off yet, but I'll certainly bear it in mind, with cake like this," Parlour laughed.

"Look, you're the detective, but if I were you, I would maybe return to Kat Jankowiczowa's flat. But I would also interview any other employees in social housing. I would not concentrate so much on Billock Towers – in my view, the kidnapper would not implicate themselves by asking for the ransom to be left so near their accommodation. I think they probably live in a council flat or house somewhere else in the area."

"That all sounds logical, Olga," Parlour nodded. "I do appreciate your input. You're wasted in interpreting – you know that?"

They exchanged small talk whilst enjoying the lusciously moist cakes home-baked on the premises. It was a welcome respite from the tension at Billock CID.

31

On return to the station, Parlour had a quick word with Superintendent Dewhurst before calling DS Goodlove to his office. Goodlove was ordered to check out the addresses of all BestCo employees to ascertain which postcodes were located within social housing schemes, or less desirable areas of town. He would then pay these employees a visit and double-check their alibis for the days in question. Goodlove was also to query whether any of them were aware of other colleagues who may have abused personal data laws or who may have a particular grudge against individual customers or certain customer profiles.

Parlour decided to take a uniformed officer along with him to Billock Towers. Constable Nick Fairbrass could snoop around the flat for evidence of a computer and printer whilst Parlour kept Kat Jankowiczowa occupied. Whilst there was no way Jankowiczowa could have accessed BestCo's server from a private broadband account, there was no reason why she couldn't have printed the ransom notes from her home address – assuming, that was, Kat had had anything to do with the abductions in the first place.

Within half an hour, Parlour was inside the dank lift-shaft of Billock Towers high-rise, trying not to breathe in the foul smell of stale urine and last weekend's vomit as he ascended to the 15th floor with Fairbrass.

"Mrs Jankowiczowa? Sorry to bother you again," Parlour smiled, as a pale and harassed Kat opened the door to Billock CID once more.

"I'm Detective Chief Inspector Mark Parlour and this is Police Constable Nick Fairbrass, Billock CID."

"Sent the big boss in now, have they?" Kat said sarcastically, standing to one side to let them squeeze past her and into the living room.

"I'm not the Senior Investigating Officer on this case, actually. And I'm not here to antagonize you; I just need to ask you a few questions. Is your husband in?"

Jankowiczowa shook her head sullenly. "He's taken the children to the play-park. They didn't go to school today. You see how my whole family is being affected by this nonsense."

How convenient, Parlour thought. Grygor must have received word that the police were in the building. Jankowiczowa's hostile stance was not lost on Parlour.

"You're the one who visited my friend Aleks, aren't you?" Jankowiczowa stated, leading the way. "Aleksandra Kowalewa."

It would help if she didn't make every word sound like an accusation, Parlour thought to himself.

"Yes, I did, nice place she has there," he replied, noting her facial expression.

"Aleks and Jan have... how do you say it? Fallen on their feet?"

"*Landed* on their feet," Parlour corrected her, accepting a seat on a very saggy sofa shoved up against the wall of the cluttered flat. Fairbrass sat opposite on a well-scuffed faux leather tub-chair. It was clear to Parlour from the shadow that crossed her face alone that she was exceedingly bitter at how life had turned out for her in England.

"I would offer you a coffee, but I'm out of milk. Haven't had a chance today to do the shopping," Jankowiczowa said acerbically.

"Of course you haven't," Parlour replied kindly, attempting a conciliatory smile. He could have informed her that he took his coffee black in any case, but didn't feel like another shot of caffeine so soon after Gianni's full roast rocket fuel, and especially not from one of her mugs, if the stained, chipped variety on the table were anything to go by. Besides, it was hardly likely to be ground coffee, even if they were continental Europeans.

"So why are you here? I have nothing else to say to you. I've already told your Sergeant that I had nothing to do with these missing ladies."

Parlour paused. He needed to exercise extreme caution here and play it just right. "I was wondering, Mrs Jankowiczowa – Kat - if you could do me a favour."

"What could I possibly do for you?" Jankowiczowa sneered mistrustfully. Did Parlour imagine it, or did he fleetingly spot fear in her eyes?

Parlour took a deep breath. "We're pretty sure that an employee of BestCo is involved in the abduction of Lorraine Girding and Eve Beckford and the attempted abduction of Mrs Juliet Parlour, my wife. My wife is adamant she heard someone say the word or name Kat on a number of occasions. You have to admit, we have to question you on the basis of that evidence."

"I suppose," Jankowiczowa conceded.

"However," Parlour began, offering the sugared pill to her, "It is my belief that a British person is behind the kidnappings. I believe you are innocent, Mrs Jankowiczowa – Kat."

"Do you really?" Jankowiczowa asked, a flicker of hope in her voice.

Parlour nodded. "However, to get my boss, the Senior Investigating Officer on this case, off my back, and therefore off your back, there's something you can do for me now."

"Please, just tell me."

"Would you just let Nick here search your flat? Then, because we'll find nothing, we can eliminate you from our enquiries and leave you alone once and for all."

There was a long pause, in which Jankowiczowa stared at Parlour, clearly unsure of whether she should trust him or not. Finally she looked away towards the grimy window.

"And you will leave me alone if you find nothing?"

Parlour nodded, hoping fervently that the gamble would pay off. He had to admit, he was not entirely convinced of her innocence. There was something fishy about her whole demeanour, that could not be explained away by nerves or insecurity. She clearly seemed to be weighing something up in her mind.

"OK then," Jankowiczowa replied finally. "Be my guest."

Parlour gave Fairbrass the nod and sat uneasily on the sofa, pretending to be occupied with incoming messages on his Blackberry whilst keeping a close eye on Jankowiczowa, who was also feigning business in the kitchen. Fortunately the kitchen area was only separated from the living room by a simple archway; Parlour could easily keep an unobtrusive eye on the potential suspect.

It didn't take too long for Fairbrass to return from the two bedrooms, bathroom and hallway area; he then began a thorough search of the living room before Jankowiczowa allowed him access to the small, cluttered kitchen area.

Fairbrass motioned to Parlour that he needed a word and Parlour slipped out into the hallway with him, shutting the living room door behind him.

"Not a sign of a computer, laptop or printer, boss," Fairbrass whispered. "But I did find this..."

The constable held out a small USB device in his gloved hand.

"What is it, some kind of memory stick?" Parlour asked.

"It's one of those Talk 21 wireless internet dongles," Fairbrass replied.

Parlour's ears pricked up. "Are you sure?"

"I've got an identical one at home, Sir."

"So she lied about the internet connection!" Parlour hissed.

"Not technically," Fairbrass replied. "They don't have an internet connection, I checked."

Parlour frowned, weighing up the most rational, if not most popular, plan of action.

"Where did you find it?"

"It was in the bedside drawer under some socks, but on her husband's side."

"Doesn't necessarily implicate him," Parlour thought aloud.

"What do you think we should do, boss?"

"We'll need to take it back to the station, Nick. She's not going to like it. There might be some information saved on it that's relevant to the case."

"He also has a thumping great pair of binoculars stashed under the bed in a shoe-box. Not sure what that's all about."

Parlour shrugged. "Bird-watching?"

"So why hide the binoculars?"

They returned to the living room. Jankowiczowa had clearly been listening through the door, as she perched unnaturally on the edge of the sofa, tea towel inexplicably scrunched up on the coffee table, as he entered.

"My constable found this wireless internet USB dongle in your husband's bedside cabinet," Parlour informed her rather sternly.

Jankowiczowa shrugged. "Did you?"

"You'll have to do better than that," Parlour said grimly, as she feigned innocence – badly.

"It belongs to Grygor. I am not my husband's keeper."

"So where's the laptop to go with it?" Parlour enquired in a tone several degrees cooler than that used in his opening gambits with the Polish woman.

"How would I know?" Jankowiczowa exclaimed, gesturing rather wildly with her hands. "My husband has it, I expect."

"At the play park?" Parlour laughed sarcastically, then wiped the grin off his own face. "Or stashed at a mate's elsewhere in this tower block, after you got word we were in the building? We can search the tower block, all twenty floors, right now, if that's how you want to play it."

"I don't know where his laptop is," Jankowiczowa said quietly. "He took it out with him this morning, you are right. But where he left it, I do not know. Perhaps he still has it.

Perhaps he is playing games on it in the park. You know what men are like when you ask them to look after the children – always one eye on the telly or the computer. In fact, I'm surprised he didn't take the TV to the park with him as well!"

If it was an attempt to lighten the atmosphere, it failed dismally. And neither did Parlour appreciate the barb against fathers. In his world, Juliet was the one more likely to be tapping away on the laptop whilst attempting to feed Rowan one handed, whereas he was more inclined to take total time-out from whatever adult chore he had been engaged in to spend quality time with his young son. Or at least, that was the view from his perspective.

"Where's the printer, Kat?" It was worth pushing his luck. She'd caved in over the laptop, after all.

"No printer," Jankowiczowa stated, shaking her head. Parlour stared her out. The washed-out woman gave him a baleful expression and shrugged her shoulders. "Look, I'm sorry I lied about the internet connection – but it was not a big lie. I do not use his wireless thing. It is nothing to do with me."

Could he trust her? Parlour just wasn't sure and began to understand where Goodlove was coming from. She was certainly on edge and concealing something; nevertheless, Parlour felt his initial instinct, that Grygor Jankowicz was up to something illegal entirely unconnected with the case, was still the more likely scenario.

"I'm going to have to take this wireless dongle back to the station, I'm afraid. And I also need your husband's laptop. Could you direct my constable to the play park, please? I'll wait here."

Jankowiczowa put her head in her hands in resignation. "He's probably left it at his friend Stan's - Stanislaw Grabowski. You'll find him on the floor below, Flat 4."

32

"So you found nothing incriminating on the laptop, then?" Juliet enquired, pouring her husband a small measure of wine with their evening meal, just in case the investigation into the abductions of Lorraine Girding and Eve Beckford suddenly gathered pace and Parlour was called out.

"I wouldn't go that far," Parlour replied, swirling the wine around in his glass pretentiously before testing it. Good, the wine warehouse in Foxburgh had done them proud with a fantastically fruity Sicilian red. "Nothing to do with the case, that's for sure. But every indication that he'd been browsing dodgy websites and had attempted to wipe the evidence."

He'd caught Technical Support at a good time and they'd managed to trawl through the hard drive late that afternoon.

"What, porn or worse?" Juliet frowned.

"Young girls, teenagers. Soft-core, level 3. And some fuzzy photos of the local teenage talent, by the looks of it, from his own personal collection – probably using a zoom lens from his flat window, though we didn't find a camera."

"Will you charge him for it?"

Parlour shook his head. "He just seems to have browsed the websites, not downloaded anything or paid for porn. So we can't prosecute. And the girls in the photos were fully clothed. He'll get off with a friendly warning – perhaps not so friendly. Maybe I'll set Lin Dawe on him! There's no evidence he's linked to any porn or paedo rings or anything like that. Wife possibly knew but turned a blind eye to it."

"Blimey, don't know if I would be so forgiving!" Juliet exclaimed.

"She might have thought it was relatively harmless in the grand scheme of things – looking at it from a purely secular standpoint. Better than him actually having sex with a minor, I suppose, from her perspective," Parlour said soberly. "It's a sad state of affairs when the world's so screwed up we have to take that attitude towards such things."

"Did you check out her church attendance?"

Parlour nodded. "She is indeed a regular worshipper at the Polish Orthodox in Billock. The Priest said she attends whenever possible, but that work made it difficult for her to come week in week out."

"And does the porn-addict attend too?" Juliet enquired acerbically.

Parlour shook his head, taking a large swig of his wine. "He's used life in England to escape from his homeland habits and responsibilities, it seems. Katerina plays the loyal wife and defends him to the hilt, but it doesn't take a genius to work out that there's cracks in that marriage. She's working all hours to pay the bills while he's in a low paid job hanging around with his mates on the estate."

"Ogling at girls young enough to be his daughter," Juliet interjected angrily.

"Now now, the binoculars could be for more wholesome activities," Parlour tutted humorously.

"There's only one type of bird-watching he's interested in," Juliet snorted, "The type that involves young girls in tight skirts with loose morals."

"Miaow!" Parlour grinned.

Juliet glared at him over the top of her wine glass.

"Kat seems to be pulled in every direction," Parlour continued. "But it appears her faith is still strong, at least."

"To be honest, Mark, I thought you were barking up the wrong tree with that Kat woman, anyway," Juliet commented, helping herself to a slice of pizza. With precious little time together to enjoy a healthy home-cooked meal at the moment, it was small wonder her waistline and thigh circumference showed little sign of decreasing. Whilst her body acted much like an Economy 7 heater, storing up fuel for later, Parlour, with his frantic metabolism, seemed to burn off the calories almost as he consumed them. Thus her pencil thin husband showed no signs of suffering from excess, except maybe in the facial eruptions department.

"I wasn't barking up that tree really, in any case," Parlour replied. "More sniffing at the base!"

"Ew!"

"But why do you say that?" Parlour challenged her. "What?"

"That you don't think Katerina Jankowiczowa is involved in the kidnappings?"

"There was just something bugging me about the whole cat/Kat thing. And I couldn't put my finger on it at first. But I know now why I don't think it was about this woman."

"Well then, spill the beans!"

"I can't be sure – you have to understand that it was really noisy in the van and I was still pretty groggy from the chloroform -"

"Yes, yes," Parlour hurried her along.

"It's just that the way they said "cat", I didn't feel they were talking about a *person.* "

"But they surely weren't talking about a household pet, either?"

"I'm not sure," Juliet said slowly, wrinkling her nose up as she considered her response. "It sounded more like a codename than somebody's actual name, if you know what I mean. It was just their intonation, the way they kept saying it really quickly, almost staccato. I can't explain it other than that. It's just an intuitive thing, I suppose."

"Often very accurate, nonetheless," Parlour stated, munching thoughtfully on his pepperoni and mixed pepper pizza.

"So what are you going to do now, since the Polish woman proved a dead end?"

"I have nine BestCo employees on our hit-list still to be interviewed – Goodlove couldn't get hold of them today. He's done brilliantly. There are only so many stinky Council pads you can manage in one day. I've sent him home with some laundry tablets and a Ventolin!"

"PC to the last," Juliet grinned at her husband's snobbery. "I take it there's a certain class of employee you're especially interested in?"

"I reckon this is someone with a serious grudge against the Yummy Mummy brigade. Logically, this is probably a woman who doesn't have the option of staying at home with a kid. Or someone who hasn't found a husband to give her the house and family she craves. Maybe she's infertile; more likely, she's just plain twisted. Consumed with envy."

"She?"

"Oh yes. We think it's a woman behind this, though she obviously has some red-necks assisting her – doubtlessly for a share of the readies."

"So let me get this right. You think that a woman who works for BestCo is illegally accessing customer data to abduct, or organise the abduction of, well-off stay-at-home Mums, whom she is insanely jealous of?"

"That's about it, Jules."

"So these aren't women she bumps into in the store – cos they wouldn't have their shopping delivered."

"Not her targets, no. I expect she got the idea from the kind of women she met in the store, though. Or it's just possible she used to be a BestCo delivery driver fairly recently and is familiar with the targets from her stint as a driver. But so far we've found no-one working on the shop floor who fits that spec."

"What about the current female drivers?"

"There's only two of them. One's happily married with teenage kids and lives in the next street up from your parents. The other is civil-ceremonied to another woman and currently has her leg in plaster after a ski-ing accident last month."

"Mark?"

"Yes?"

"Am I a Yummy Mummy?"

"Most definitely," Parlour grinned, and fondly squeezed his wife's chubby cheeks across the table.

33

"So in your view, Parlour," Detective Chief Superintendent Christopher Dewhurst began, five minutes into the team briefing at 9am that Friday morning, "the delectable Katerina Jankowiczowa is all but out of the picture?"

Dewhurst enunciated the Polish woman's name with exaggerated diction, imbuing the word *delectable* with a considerable degree of sarcasm.

"I wouldn't go that far, Sir," Parlour frowned, who disliked the Superintendent's inability to entertain greyness, however temporal; Dewhurst felt the need to rule everything in or out at all times. To this day, Parlour had no idea how Christopher Dewhurst had ascended to the lofty heights of Detective Superintendent. He wasn't, as far as Parlour was aware, a frequenter of the local Masonic Hall. He was, however, a wealthy man and used his platinum credit card to curry favour with the County's movers and shakers.

"We still have a negligible alibi and potential access to Customer info," Parlour continued. "Plus the testimony of my own wife concerning the word cat. We also know that Juliet complained about two women of Eastern European descent, employed at BestCo in Billock – though she was unable to reliably pick them out from staff ID photographs supplied to us by Darren Clump."

Parlour paused for breath. "That said, though, I do think we need to broaden the net, Sir. We can't assume this is a BestCo employee. And we can't take it for granted it's a woman either, despite Olga Malinowska's summation. She has an uncanny knack of being right; but I wouldn't want to lay too much store by her logic."

"So what exactly are you saying, then, Parlour?" Dewhurst clicked impatiently. "Shall we just go ahead and interview the entire blinkin' socially housed population of South East Hampshire?"

"I was just making a point, Sir, that time's ticking on and we're no closer to finding the two women – I still think the link between them is BestCo home delivery, but it could all be a coincidence. "

"OK, OK, point taken, Parlour," Dewhurst sighed heavily. "There's no news on the white Transit, I take it?"

Sean Denton shook his head. "Masses of Hampshire 53 and 58 registered transits to wade through, but nothing sus as yet. It's a shame we don't have more numbers or letters to go on."

"I'd say it's pretty hard to memorize a number plate when you've a knife at your throat," Parlour commented sarcastically, in defence of his wife.

Denton tipped his head in assent.

"What about the garage forecourts – I thought someone was checking through the CCTV footage for white transits filling up?" Parlour persevered.

Denton blew his cheeks out. "The boys were still working on it last time I checked. It's a big call – there's a heck of a lot of service stations between here and Pompey and they could have filled up anytime this week."

"Not good enough, Sean," Parlour said tightly, looking his junior colleague briefly in the eye. "This is a potential murder investigation. Need I remind you that these women have been missing for a week and a half? Senior staff have to work all hours; I expect junior colleagues to pull their weight as well."

"Received and understood, Sir," Denton muttered, looking down at the floor.

"Goodlove, I believe you're checking out more checkout girls today?" Dewhurst queried.

"I wouldn't quite phrase it that way, Sir," Goodlove frowned, thinking of the pasty-faced till operators he'd faced yes terday. What was it with so many young girls these days, that they were either grotesquely over-weight, or terribly malnourished, their white scabby faces pinched and scowling, skin further tautened by the scraped back lank hair look? If yesterday's BestCo employees were anything to go by, Goodlove truly was glad to be batting rear guard! Mind you, that BestCo Shopfloor Manager, Darren Clump, was a bit of male eye candy, even if he did sound like a right muppet with a name like that.

Goodlove consulted his wristwatch. "Actually, Sir, I better make a move now. My first interview is lined up for 9.30 – lady by the delightful name of Courtney Brimstock, also known as The Broomstick. Bit of a witch, by all accounts."

"Better check out her coven, then, Cam," Parlour laughed, sense of humour restored now that his wife's life was not in danger.

Dewhurst grunted. "Let's plough on with the leads we do have, then. I want to know the *second* any of you have something of relevance."

He left for his office. Parlour rose his eyebrows and returned to his own desk. Pouring himself a fresh mug of black coffee from his filter jug, he sifted carelessly through the case notes on his desk. *Darnit.* He couldn't sit here all day waiting for Goodlove to bring back the results of the staff interviews. Parlour stood up and beckoned Preece into his office.

"Karen – can you take over the forecourt footage? Sorry, bit menial, I know, but sometimes the organ-grinder has a better eye for detail than the monkeys."

Parlour's DI made a face. "Thanks a bunch. Is that my penance for..."

"Don't," Parlour interjected quietly. "It never happened, remember?"

Preece nodded. There was an awkward moment before Parlour slipped his overcoat on.

"I'm off to rattle some cages at Billock Towers. Can't sit around here twiddling my thumbs all day. Maybe I'll have another poke around Fryer's Dip, as well."

34

Parlour was just returning to his car at 4pm, following a frustrating and fruitless door knocking session at Billock Towers, when the call came through from Karen Preece.

Having left his Constable to finish off the bottom three floors of the high-rise, Parlour was only too grateful to relax in the comfortable leather seats of his sports car and hear what was hopefully some good news at long last. He could get some junior officers to pay Fryer's Dip another visit tomorrow.

"Boss, I've spotted something on those tapes."

"Our transit van?"

"Oh, plenty of those, but all legit and accounted for."

"What then?" Parlour asked impatiently.

"I've found footage of our friend Kat - wait for it - on the evening of Wednesday 9th of November."

"Katerina Jankowiczowa filling up at a service station the day Lorraine Girding was abducted? But she doesn't even drive a car!" Parlour exclaimed.

"Not filling up with fuel, boss. Topping up her mobile at BP on West Street."

"In Billock town centre?"

"Yep, at 8.55 pm. It's definitely her. And – get this – she leaves the kiosk with a toy-boy in tow!"

"What! But she's..."

"A downtrodden good Catholic married mother of two? She strung us along nicely, didn't she? Cam reckoned there was something sus about her, turns out he was right."

"Hold on, hold on," Parlour stopped her, unwilling to concede too much ground at this juncture. "There could be a perfectly innocent explanation, though granted she's already lied to us about her whereabouts on that evening."

"There's more, boss," Karen continued, on a roll now.

"What then?"

"I asked Lynda Miles to take a look. As press officer, she knows half the county, doesn't she? Anyway, just happens she's put her flat on the market recently."

"So what?" Parlour barked impatiently.

"So she's had estate agents smarming round her apartment touting for business. The guy with Jankowiczowa works for Brentfields in Billock High Street – that new agency. An independent, I think. He's an estate agent. About half her age. Goes by the name of Jason – greasy little oik, by all accounts."

"An estate agent?" Parlour echoed, brain clicking into overdrive. An estate agent would have access to properties and a knowledge of the local area. Could it be that the abductions were a team effort? But if so, what on earth was the motive? It just didn't make sense. What could a thirty-something Polish migrant mother of two possibly have in common with a callow young estate agent from Billock? And what link could they realistically have with the abducted women? Yet it could not be denied, an estate agent was the one person who might have instant access to the properties in question. And blimey, Parlour suddenly thought, slapping the dashboard in excited agitation, Brentfields began with a B. Could it possibly be that both Lorraine Girding and Eve Beckford had made an appointment with Brentfields to have their properties valued? Was that the link?

He would have to check with their respective partners to see if either had plans of moving. It made no sense that either couple should seek to sell such top-end properties at this stage in their family lives; yet Parlour knew couples with no focus beyond this earthly kingdom were rarely satisfied with what they had. There was always another step to be taken on the ladder of social status. It didn't quite ring true, but there were too many coincidences for Parlour to ignore.

He sighed. Kat Jankowiczowa was an enigma. Just when he felt he'd made a firm decision to eliminate her from their enquiries, she wriggled into the frame once more. He'd seen way too much of her pasty face for his liking these past few days.

"Get her in straightaway, Karen. I'll be back in ten."

There was just time to make a couple of phone calls to Girding and Beckford. Reluctantly, Parlour turned the key in the ignition and headed back to HQ.

But Kat was nowhere to be found.

35

Detective Chief Superintendent Dewhurst could barely contain his glee on discovering Katerina Jankowiczowa had gone AWOL.

"It should be relatively easy to round up the Pole," Dewhurst commented rather crassly to Parlour in the Incident Room.

Heil Hitler, Parlour thought to himself, frowning. The woman was probably fed up to her back teeth of Billock CID and scared to death of being framed for a series of crimes she didn't commit. Parlour couldn't blame her for absconding, in the circumstances. This time, the handbag, keys and mobile phone were not found at the property, suggesting Jankowiczowa had left of her own accord. Grygor Jankowicz had revealed that his wife had left their flat at around 10 am that morning to go to work and had not returned. But she had not clocked in at work that morning and neither Grygor nor any of her colleagues at BestCo had an inkling where she could have got to. Parlour was not convinced that Grygor would have bothered reporting her absence, in any case – or perhaps only when his stomach started to protest.

Aleks Kowalewa had already been questioned and claimed to have heard nothing from Kat. Rather suspiciously though, Parlour thought, she had even proffered her mobile phone for inspection to the DC who'd visited her at home in Chave. But that proved nothing. Parlour wouldn't have been surprised if both women had purchased new PAYG phones following the recent bouts of police questioning. A quick search of Jan Kowal's property revealed no new lodgers - however, that again proved little. No-one would be naive enough to hide their best friend in their own home.

The ports and airports were already under alert for signs of women in wheelchairs; now a photo of Katerina

Jankowiczowa, supplied courtesy of BestCo Billock West, could be added to the surveillance operation.

Detective Sergeant Goodlove shared Dewhurst's view that Katerina was involved in the abductions; thus her impromptu disappearance only served to strengthen their convictions. DI Preece was more circumspect, sharing Parlour's doubts regarding Kat's motivation to have committed the crimes in question. This was an accusation, Karen Preece felt, groaning under the weight of circumstantial evidence.

With nothing to do but wait for news of Kat's whereabouts, Parlour decided to bunk off early. Juliet's recent abduction and the marital reunification that had followed, had reawakened Parlour's desire to spend time with his young family.

Parlour briefly filled Juliet in on the latest developments; it seemed only fair given her direct involvement in the case. Anyhow, he trusted her implicitly not to breathe a word about it to anyone. Whilst Juliet could be opinionated by mouth and mercurial by temperament, she was never indiscreet.

A very tasty home-cooked vegetarian cannelloni followed. Fed up of junk food and takeaways, Juliet had walked the twenty minutes it took to reach the local supermarket in Deverton, where she had deliberately given the convenience foods aisle a wide berth and opted for fresh ingredients instead. Things were definitely looking up - Juliet had even taken the time to whizz up some spinach, tomatoes and pasta in the blender to make a nutritious veggie concoction for little Rowan. A feeling of calm and serenity presided in the Parlour household, despite Parlour's own frustrations at the lack of progress on the abductions enquiry.

A couple of hours later, Rowan was bathed, talced and tucked up in bed with Grunty the grubby piglet. Parlour was just putting some picture books back on the shelf when his eyes were drawn to a nightlight Juliet had recently plugged in next to the cot. It seemed to protrude quite far out of the wall. Parlour had not really noticed before; he reached over and extracted the light. He then realised why it wasn't plugged in flush to the wall; the actual night-light had a European two-pin fitting and was attached to a three pin adaptor plug. Parlour recalled that Juliet's father had picked it up at a car boot for a pound – they'd admonished him at the time for wasting money on it, but true to form, Juliet had managed to find a use for the adaptor.

As Parlour plugged it back in again, he felt a tingling sensation in his temples. Something suddenly struck him as being potentially important. He hurtled downstairs and clicked open his briefcase. Rummaging around, he found the copies he had taken of the ransom photo. He got a magnifying glass out of the pocket in the inside lid and held it over the picture. Yes, there was no doubt about it.... that was a British electrical socket in the wall of the kidnappers' dank hiding place. Why hadn't anyone spotted it before? Probably because it was nothing out of the ordinary – the eye simply skimmed over familiar detail without questioning it.

Lorraine Girding and Eve Beckford were not being held in France, unless this was some kind of holding station *en route* to the continent. There was a slim possibility this was some hideout in France with British sockets attached, but it was generally only holiday homes popular with British tourists that boasted both European and British electrical points, not dingy old garages and outbuildings. So where the heck were they?

Parlour decided to get on the phone to Portsmouth Police immediately. Perhaps the women were being held locally in a garage or cellar before being smuggled over to the continent. He'd flex some muscle and get some local coppers to make a renewed search of garages and outbuildings.

36

Rather predictably, Katerina Jankowiczowa was found holed up in the flat of a fellow Pole just around the corner in the Trees Estate, a rundown 60s housing estate a short bus-ride away from Billock Towers.

Once uniform had rounded her up and deposited her back at Billock Station, which was fast becoming her second home, Dewhurst had got to work on her. The Superintendent was determined to beat a confession out of her where Parlour had so far failed.

Dewhurst's more bludgeoning approach yielded little to progress the investigation. Kat had admitted to a brief fling with Jason Deakin, whom she had met across the checkout at BestCo. There'd been no sex, just an aborted trip to a city centre boozer on the Wednesday in question. He'd met her off the bus in West Street at about ten to nine. As her mobile phone was running low, she'd dragged him into the BP petrol station nearby to top up before going to the rather rundown Prince of Wales, or Price o Wals as it stood, its signage in a state of permanent disrepair. Deakin had suggested the pub as they would be unlikely to meet anyone they knew; Jankowiczowa had realised rather bitterly some time after that Deakin had no concerns for her welfare, he was simply too embarrassed to tout her around the smarter chain pubs he usually frequented with his single friends.

When she had refused to accompany him to a vacant property on his books for sex, he had made an excuse to leave. Feeling cheap and foolish, Jankowiczowa had returned home to her husband and kids and gone straight to bed.

It was a sad little story and despite Dewhurst's misgivings, the observing Parlour was inclined to believe her. The greasy little toe rag from Brentfields had clearly seen a chance for some casual sex; sometimes he despaired of his own gender. What was more, neither the Girdings nor the Beckfords had entertained any recent ideas of re-entering the property market according to both spouses of the missing women. Girding stated that his wife would never arrange such an appointment behind his back. Beckford stated that they had briefly considered moving house about a year ago but had decided against it in the current financial climate and had voted to redecorate instead – hence Eve Beckford's current painting project.

It was just as Parlour thought; Deakin and Kat had absolutely zilch in common and no motive whatsoever for abducting the two women. She was fed up of her depressing little existence in Billock Towers high-rise; Deakin, like many young men, was at the mercy of his genitals. Their respective needs had collided across a conveyor belt and they'd met up to scratch the itch. In the end, Jankowiczowa had returned home itchy, Deakin found relief elsewhere.

Thoroughly depressed by the whole tawdry affair, Parlour decided to leave Dewhurst to bang his bald pate against a brick wall. Whilst Jankowiczowa was not out of the woods yet, Parlour felt there was far more to be gained by exploring other options. In his view, there had been far too much energy expended on rounding up disaffected Poles than pursuing the primary goal of discovering the whereabouts of Lorraine Girding and Eve Beckford.

So it was with some considerable relief that Parlour encountered an excitable DS Goodlove in the station car park.

"Might have a breakthrough, Sir!" Goodlove exclaimed, alighting from his grubby black Astra and banging the car roof in triumph.

"Spill the beans then!" Parlour grinned, leaning back on his car which was parked in the special DCI bay reserved for him. It was probably the best perk of being promoted from common old DI to DCI grade.

"Well, as you know, I asked Paul Gregson, the Store Manager of BestCo to supply me with the contact details of all Billock West BestCo employees. Based on their postal addresses, I made a list of... um... socially disadvantaged employees and arranged to interview them. I had high hopes of a few of them, especially The Broomstick, but I found nothing untoward. It then hit me that we ought to check out the staff at the other branches of BestCo that provide on-line grocery deliveries. It occurred to me that they might have access to Billock West's customer database without actually working at that store."

"Yes, yes," Parlour agreed impatiently, wishing Goodlove would drop the rather irritating habit of feeding him *the story so far* instead of cutting to the chase immediately.

"So I'm sitting there on the blower to Portsmouth and Southampton branches trying to arrange for some staff details to be emailed through to me when I realise I have a missed call. I go back to it and find it's Paul Gregson, the Online Grocery Delivery Manager at Billock West."

"And?" Parlour interjected snappily, become increasingly annoyed with Goodlove and congratulating himself not for the first time for promoting Karen Preece over him.

"He left a cryptic message asking me to call him. So I did, and it only turns out that one of his members of staff has disappeared off the face of the earth."

"Someone we've already interviewed?" Parlour frowned.

Goodlove shook his head.

"Do we have a name for our mysterious vanishing woman?" Parlour asked sarcastically.

Goodlove informed him and Parlour wrote it down, pulling a face as he did so.

"I take it you've informed the Super?"

"Dewhurst went home with gut-rot after lunch, Sir. He's up to speed, but told me to hand it over to you."

Parlour grinned to himself. "Do me a favour, Goodlove. Can you ask Paul Gregson to dig out a copy of her Curriculum Vitae or her original application form for BestCo; they should still have it on file. I'm heading over to the supermarket now. Does she live alone?"

"No, boss, lives with her mother."

"Have uniform already been to her house to take some details?"

"Yes, Sir, they're there now."

"Good. Make sure their report is waiting for me on my table when I get back to the station."

"There's something else, boss," Goodlove continued triumphantly. "BestCo had failed deliveries recorded for both Lorraine Girding and Eve Beckford on the days in question."

"Good work, Cam." It was like praising a large puppy, Parlour thought to himself. He switched his Blackberry to speaker phone and headed towards the ring road that would take him out of central Billock to the western outskirts of the town.

37

An anxious looking Paul Gregson met Parlour in the entrance foyer of BestCo and led him discreetly upstairs to his office in the management suite.

"Sorry for the cloak and dagger," Gregson apologised to Parlour.

"We've had the press sniffing round here today – not great, on our busiest day of the week. Someone's let the cat out of the bag about the home delivery connection in the kidnappings."

"It's a bit too much to expect, that an entire workforce of a place like this would keep their mouths shut," Parlour nodded, taking a seat opposite him in his chilly office, where the air-con was proving rather over-effective.

"No company loyalty, that's the problem. And it's not the Poles to blame on that score," Gregson frowned. "Don't know they're born, half of them. Could learn a thing or two from the Polish ladies about hard graft."

That's what Olga Malinowska said, Parlour thought to himself, sensing more than ever that this case had nothing to do with Katerina Jankowiczowa or her buddy Aleks.

Gregson handed Parlour a rather worse for wear BestCo application form, dated 13 January 2008. Parlour scanned it quickly. He noted that the missing woman had transferred to the new store from Portsmouth branch and wondered how relevant that might be, given the direction in which the kidnappers' white transit van was heading on the day that his wife was abducted.

"And you say she didn't turn up for work today?"

Gregson nodded. "Mad Cow had the week off. But she was due in today. She's very reliable; she doesn't pull sickies. Needs the cash too much, I think."

"Mad Cow?" Parlour queried, shaking his head in puzzlement.

Gregson grinned briefly. "It's a nickname. You can see why from the application form. Kind of apt, given her personality."

Parlour looked at the missing girl's personal details and smiled briefly.

"So when was the last time.. um... Mad Cow came into work?"

"That'll be Friday last week, the 11th. She was on an early, so the 8 till 4.30 shift with an hour for lunch. But most of the girls take half an hour and finish at 4. I don't mind, so long as I have enough staff on the tills. It can get pretty busy post school-run."

"And she's definitely not at home?" Parlour checked.

"Her Mum hasn't seen her in days. Apparently that's not so unusual; she sometimes kips on the sofa at friends' houses. Mrs Entwhistle – that's her mum – thinks it was Wednesday that she last made an appearance. She grabbed a few clothes and a bit to eat, and said she would be back sometime. I don't think theirs was a particularly close relationship."

"Hmm," Parlour exhaled, brain ticking away furiously as he digested the potential relevance of this new information.

"I need to take a copy of this form," Parlour stated a moment later, leafing through the application. He had already spotted something of note.

"What about a car – did she drive to work?"

"That I doubt very much," Gregson replied, a picture of the untidy, down-at-heel young lady springing to mind. "There's an excellent bus service here from Billock, where most of the girls live, and we find the vast majority come by bus. There aren't many girls work here can afford to run their own cars – though we hope to help them out of the spiral of debt most have got themselves into."

Aww, the caring face of the corporate giant, Parlour thought sarcastically to himself.

"Do you have a photo of the missing girl?"

"Yep. This is Mad Cow," Gregson obliged, handing Parlour a mug-shot of an overweight young girl, set against a white backdrop – evidently some kind of in-store ID Card photo shoot. Parlour peered at the pudgy girl in the photograph. She was scowling at the camera.

"And you say she works on the tills?"

"She does now."

"She didn't always?" Parlour enquired, ears pricking up.

"We had her on home delivery for a while, but a customer complained about her. Apparently Mad Cow was a bit rude to some stuck-up biddy in Chave Hamlets. We disciplined her, but we didn't want to lose her. She's not too easy on the eye, but she's a grafter, so we trained her up on the tills instead. Believe me, when you find someone who isn't afraid of a bit of hard work and has no kiddie issues to get in the way, then they become like gold-dust in a place like this. It's the age-old problem of working with a large female workforce – and believe you me, most of them are large, ha ha." Gregson laughed rather unpleasantly at his own joke. "Women are always leaving to have babies, and when they come back, they spend half the time dashing off to attend to them. Are you married, DCI Parlour?"

"I have a wife and baby son, yes," Parlour said proudly. He couldn't help it; he just felt inordinately proud of being father to a son. He was not sure if he would feel quite the same about a little girl, though he sensed his wife would have preferred a daughter to fuss over and cosset. "But she stays at home with the nipper."

"Quite right, too, in my view," Gregson commented, with a clarity of vision that suggested he had suffered greatly from the complicated lives of working women in his charge.

"If you can afford it," Parlour conceded. Fortunately, they were in a position to give Rowan that privilege of a parent permanently on tap. Parlour stood up to go. "Just one more thing, Mr Gregson."

"Yes?"

"Would you say Mad Cow was a popular member of staff or was she a bit of a loner?"

"Why are you talking in the past tense?" Gregson enquired, paling once more. "You surely don't think she's been..."

"No, no," Parlour interjected hastily, realising Gregson was assuming Mad Cow was the victim, not the perpetrator.

"She did her own thing, but she wasn't a loner, if that makes any sense," Gregson replied after some consideration. "I mean, she didn't need to have her coffee break at the same time as her mates. She didn't do everything in pairs like lots of women do. I swear that some of them still trot off to the loo together well into their 50s! She didn't dance round anyone's handbag, put it that way."

"So her own woman. Neither popular nor unpopular?" Parlour surmised.

Gregson made a face and shrugged. "I'd say most people think she's a grumpy moo but recognise that she works hard. She's always willing to swap shifts and stuff like that, too, which is appreciated and tends to make most staff keep on the right side of her. I get the impression that she needs the money or is keen to rake in as much cash as possible. She looks like she could do with it, if you know what I mean."

"No boyfriends?"

"I shouldn't think so," Gregson replied, looking aghast at the mere thought of a physical relationship with the unpleasant looking woman in question. "But she keeps herself to herself; I don't know a great deal about her."

We'll see what the Police Computer has to say about Mad Cow, Parlour thought to himself, putting his coat on. "Well, you've been very helpful anyway. Thanks. We'll be in touch as soon as we know anything."

<h1 style="text-align:center">38</h1>

Parlour returned to the station to find a pile of outstanding paperwork on his desk. Shutting the door to indicate that he didn't wish to be disturbed, he poured himself a much needed cup of black coffee and sat down to sift through the wads of paper.

But his attention was immediately diverted by a large lime-green post-it note stuck to his flat-screen monitor. Normally this would infuriate the fastidious Parlour, whose preciousness reached new heights... or was that depths?... when it came to desk clutter.

Your wife's after you! Your mobile's turned off! Parlour recognised Denton's schoolboy scrawl. He clicked in frustration, pulling his Blackberry from his coat pocket and realising that it was indeed as dead as a doornail. Parlour got an outside line on his desk phone and Juliet answered on the second ring.

"You were after me?"

"I remembered something that might be important. It probably isn't and it seems really trivial, but I thought I should tell you."

"What then?"

"You said you were now looking for British girls with chips on their shoulders. Well, the last time I went shopping at BestCo – the same day I moaned to the Manager about those Polish women, I was served by this really rude lump of a girl on the till. I don't think she uttered a single word to me; she more or less threw my shopping at me, didn't offer to help with the packing like they usually do when you've got a baby in tow. When I'd paid and was walking off, I said "Nothing like service with a smile" or something of that ilk."

"Did she say anything back?"

"No, not as far as I know, but I was already walking away from her. She may have done."

"Don't suppose you noticed if she had a name badge on?"

"As it happens, she did. I know that because while I was waiting to load my shopping on the belt, I was just thinking, what a lump of a girl, bet she's got some silly name like Kylie or Courtney or something that doesn't suit her in the least. And when I got close up, I nearly snorted out loud, because her name was..."

"Britney?" Parlour enquired, heart beating a little faster.

"Yes!"

Shame you couldn't have remembered a few days earlier, though, Parlour thought to himself, before Britney Skinner-Entwhistle – BSE - had a chance to jump ship – literally.

"And from your brief dealings with this woman, how would you describe her, apart from lumpy with a daft name?"

"Nasty," Juliet replied immediately. "She had really nasty little eyes, like she was sizing me up and making all sorts of vicious little judgements about me."

The irony in his wife's attitude to Britney "Mad Cow" Skinner was not lost on Parlour. He exchanged a few more words before putting the phone down.

A quick phone call to Sean Denton established that Britney Skinner or Entwhistle had no police record. What next? It couldn't be ruled out that Skinner had gone on one almighty bender over the weekend and simply hadn't returned home yet. Or that Skinner had finally had enough of her depressing little existence working the tills at BestCo and had sought pastures new without so much as a by-your-leave to anyone.

Parlour glanced briefly through the Missing Persons report and Britney Skinner's BestCo application form, before picking up the phone to Superintendent Dewhurst. After enquiring briefly after his senior colleague's health, Parlour obtained permission to organise a manhunt for the till operator known as Mad Cow. It seemed an extreme course of action but could they afford to sit back and build a case against Skinner, whilst she made off with the readies and possibly the lives of two women?

A photo of Britney Skinner would be circulated to all the ports. Officers would be sent to Skinner's old address and place of work in Portsmouth in the hope of tracking down this potentially dangerous young woman. Parlour hoped also to uncover the temporary holding station where he believed the two women were being kept.

Could it be that Billock CID had a genuine suspect at long last?

39

It was nine pm before Parlour got away from the station and back to Juliet for a late supper that cold Saturday evening in November.

"We really must get back to healthy living!" Parlour grinned, pouring out the contents of an Indian takeaway he had picked up at Deverton Triangle on the way home. The healthy eating resolution had lasted all of twenty-four hours.

"Oh come on, Mark," Juliet scoffed, taking a large sip of her red wine. "You've had a hell of a day, and I'm in no mood for cooking at this time of night. Besides, it's Saturday."

"Fair enough," Parlour smiled, kissing her head.

"So tell me all about this Mad Cow character."

"Do I have to, when I'm eating?" Parlour groaned, carrying his dinner through to the living room on a tray.

They settled down with their wine and curries in front of some tennis highlights on Sky Sport. Neither of the Parlours were fans of Saturday night television. Both of them suffered from a pathological hatred of so-called reality shows which bore no resemblance to either of their realities. They were even less fond of nasty talent shows with their formulaic manipulation of brainless wannabes. It was therefore prudent to bring Juliet up to speed on the case against the neutral backdrop of some European tennis highlights, as neither of them were tempted to throw the contents of their dinner plates at the expensive plasma screen TV!

Parlour filled her in on the sad and bitter story of Britney Skinner-Entwhistle. Her parents had split when she was just ten. Geoff Entwhistle, a car mechanic, had then married a rich widow by the name of Sheila, whom he'd been seeing on the sly during the latter years of his relationship with Anita Skinner. Entwhistle had then moved into Sheila's luxury flat at swanky Sandbanks in Dorset, home to rich stock-brokers and football managers, leaving Anita Skinner and her young daughter destitute. Unable to survive financially on his maintenance money alone, Ms Skinner (perhaps prophetically, they had never married) was forced to sell their smart three bed detached just outside of Foxburgh. Anita and young Britney then took on a small rented flat not far from Anita's place of work in Portsmouth, which remained their home until this day. Unable to deal with her parents' break-up, Britney had hidden herself in her pokey bedroom, losing herself in pop music and obsessing over unattainable film stars. Her weight problems had begun at this time, too, and many a time Anita Skinner had found a stash of chocolate wrappers stuffed inside the pillow slip or in other barely concealed hiding places in the tiny bedroom.

Britney had left school at the earliest opportunity, despite her teachers predicting a bright future if she knuckled down and actually put the effort in. She had taken a supermarket job close to home, finally ending up at the new BestCo in Billock West.

"Why fork out to travel all the way over here, when she could have stayed local? Can't be that hard up," Juliet mused.

"It's only fifteen miles or so, and the bus links are good. We know a few customers complained about her over at Pompey; I guess she fancied a fresh start," Parlour replied.

"So you think that she's your kidnapper?" Juliet enquired.

Parlour nodded, mopping up his curry with his naan. "We think she's the ringleader, yes. Olga Malinowska, the Polish interpreter, felt we were looking for a British girl with a deep-seated hatred of women who have it all – the husband, the house, the child, the financial security to stay at home. Her mother had to scrimp and save just to keep them in fish fingers."

"And probably *value* fish fingers at that," Juliet laughed. But she soon sobered up. It was a sad little story which hopefully didn't have too tragic an ending.

"I certainly felt as if she hated *me*," Juliet continued thoughtfully. "She didn't coo over Rowan or remark on his hair, which was unusual. But she wasn't just disinterested, she seemed to really dislike us, and I suppose that's what got my hackles up."

"From looking at her CV and from interviewing her mother myself earlier this evening, the pieces do fit. But if it is true, then what a tragic waste of a bright girl. This is a teenager with 8 GCSEs, with A grades in English and Maths, who had to kiss goodbye to her future just to keep the family afloat. It just shows what a desperate effect parental break-up can have on a child's future."

Parlour paused for a moment in sober contemplation of the dreadful error of judgement he had made in the front seat of his car with Karen Preece.

"So you think it was Britney who hacked into the BestCo customer database and accessed the online grocery info?" Juliet queried.

Parlour made a dubious face. "I'm not sure if she would have quite had the brains or opportunity for that; I've got one of my team delving into her personal life to find a family member or acquaintance with the nous to break into BestCo's systems – or direct access to them. However, she was certainly capable of penning those nasty ransom notes. They were well-written with no spelling mistakes – we know she was good at English. You'd be surprised just how many atrociously spelt ransom notes we come across! And the breakfast cereal certainly points to the supermarket connection – can't believe now that I didn't spot it before! But I think she probably had a helper to assist with the logistics of it all – the grubby henchmen are two a penny. I expect she paid them a decent cut for their role in all of this, but I reckon there must be someone else helping her, probably at the holding point."

"Any ideas?"

"The team are onto it now – ringing around past employees and checking out friends and neighbours."

"Do you think the women are still alive?"

Parlour nodded slowly. "I think so. I don't think the aim is to kill them; I would guess she just wants to shock them and make them suffer a bit. Take them right out of their comfort zone."

"Well, she's certainly done that!" Jules exclaimed. "So this isn't really a murder enquiry?"

"Not at the moment, no. But if we can't find these women soon, I do fear for their lives. It's been over two weeks now."

"And you have no idea where they are? Thought you were assuming they'd been stuck on a ferry to France?"

"Well, it was you who spotted an A-Z of Northern France... and the vehicle *was* heading towards the ferry ports, so it was a natural conclusion to arrive at. However, we have absolutely no sightings of them," Parlour continued, "plus the colour photo of Lorraine Girding has an English socket point on the wall behind her. That suggests they are in all probability being held in this country – though admittedly that could just be temporarily."

"So you have people out searching for them now?"

"Yep. We're concentrating in and around her haunts in Pompey, but I've sent people to scout around her childhood stomping ground near Foxburgh just in case."

"Are you sure she's not another victim?"

"She doesn't fit the spec, does she?" Parlour replied. "Whereas she does very much match our suspect ID of an angry single woman, in a low-paid job with no prospects."

"So what now?"

"Wait for a lead," Parlour replied. "Dewhurst's taken the reins this evening; he's recovered from his dodgy stomach."

Juliet laughed as her husband delved into the foil takeaway carton and stuffed an onion bhaji into his mouth whole.

40

A thoroughly defeated CID team assembled in the Incident Room at a special meeting convened for 10am that Sunday morning. Despite working through the night in an attempt to trace the whereabouts of Britney Skinner, nobody had seen hide nor hair of her since Wednesday morning, when she had made a brief appearance at home to grab some clothes. Door to door enquiries in and around Skinner's neighbourhood had yielded no results, and a thorough search of lock-ups and miscellaneous outbuildings had produced no evidence of habitation by the abducted women. Whatever technology Britney Skinner-Entwhistle had used to process and print the ransom notes, it wasn't kept at her mother's house. Darren Clump, Britney's Line Manager at BestCo, had already informed them that checkout operators had no access to computers and printers at work. The doors to the office suites had coded entry for members of the administration and management teams; till operators had their own rest area downstairs and had no need to venture upstairs.

CCTV tapes at local service stations had now been viewed, and footage from the ferry ports had been reviewed in an attempt to spot a white Hampshire registered transit van with a 53 or 58 plate driven by two shaven-headed men. Whilst there were white 53 and 58 plate vans aplenty and shaven-headed men in abundance, there were no direct hits.

CID had also drawn a blank with both the local bus company and South West trains. As Skinner was not a car-driver, it was highly likely she had availed herself of public transport during the period in question. It was therefore assumed that Skinner had been picked up by an accomplice somewhere just beyond the supermarket site, as she had not made a cameo on any CCTV cameras outside the main foyer.

Neither had she been spotted in either the customer or staff car-parks. She had in all probability left via a small staff entrance to the rear of the building and crossed over to the other side of the industrial estate, where she was picked up in a waiting car.

"She might look a biscuit barrel full of them," Dewhurst quipped, with little concession to his own bulging waistline, "but this girl is one smart cookie!"

"Where the flippin' eck has she got to? And what the flamin' eck has she done with these women?" Sean Denton enquired less eruditely.

"Get some coffees and biscuits sent up, will you, Jenkins," Dewhurst barked at his DC, all that talk of cookies whetting his appetite. "We need a serious brainstorming session. Make sure it's proper Digestives this time, none of your value muck."

Parlour reached for his Blackberry, which was vibrating in his pocket. "I have a Yorkie restraint," he said cryptically, returning to the team after taking the call.

"A small lead," Karen Preece explained for the benefit of the team, more in tune to Parlour's quirky sense of humour. "So what do you have for us?"

"It may be entirely irrelevant, but it's worth pursuing in the absence of anything else."

"What then?" Dewhurst exclaimed in exasperation.

"I just received a call from a former workmate of Britney's, from BestCo in Pompey. Reckons Britney used to have a mate she met up with at the pub now and again. Thinks he worked down at the docks somewhere. She couldn't remember his name, but said he was tall and lanky with dyed blonde hair and ....um... a zitty complexion."

The rest of the team looked away from Parlour.

"Do we know where he worked, or what pub they met up at?" Dewhurst queried.

"That's all the info she had for me, I'm afraid," Parlour replied.

"So it's just possible our spotty friend works at the ferry port and helped her smuggle the women across the Channel?" Dewhurst stated.

"Possible, yes," Parlour nodded, "though it's all rather sketchy. Guess it's worth asking around the nearest pubs and checking out the staff down at the Cross-Channel Ferry Port – though this is going back a few years, and I would have thought that sort of environment experiences a pretty high turnover of staff. It's the kind of place where students work for the summer, isn't it?"

"I wouldn't know," Karen Preece replied dryly. "I've never been a student."

"Woo-hoo!" Sean Denton exclaimed girlishly. "Just hark at Britney Skinner here!"

They all chuckled, glad for a moment's respite. It had been a frustrating morning so far.

41

Eve Beckford opened her aching eyes and adjusted to the sunshine that streaked through the dirty garage window. She looked around the room. Breakfast had been placed to one side of her, her ties just loose enough to enable her to reach a hand out and bring some food to her lips. Some more of that awful white sliced bread and a value yoghurt, with a glass of sickly sweet orange squash. She reached a tentative hand out and touched the bread. It was hard around the edges, as if it had lain there for hours. She looked at her watch – it was just after 9am. She had slept well that night. It would just have to do; she needed to eat something to keep her strength up; complaining would get her nothing but a slap in the face from the fat woman who'd appeared over the weekend.

Eve sniffed. There was a slightly metallic smell to accompany the oily, damp smell of the garage where Lorraine and herself were locked up. She looked across to Lorraine and it was then that she realised where the strange smell was coming from. Eve gasped in horror. The older lady's wrists were splattered with blood, which had dripped onto the floor and had been partially absorbed by the concrete surface. Next to the pool of blood was the metal clip of a biro.

Eve closed her eyes. *No, no, no, no, no!* She opened them again and forced herself to look at the other woman. Her face was deathly pale, her eyes shut. Did she imagine it, or was her chest still moving? Was she still alive? Oh dear God, please let her be breathing! Eve reached her left hand out but could get it nowhere near Lorraine's limp body. She wriggled and wriggled, but it was no use; she'd been tied up in such a way that the two women could neither touch nor in any way aid one another's escape.

If Lorraine wasn't dead already, she soon would be, Eve knew. There was still live blood trickling from the incisions in her wrists. Their beanpole keeper or the fat lady boss must have dropped a pen near Lorraine, whilst placing her breakfast beside her. Seizing the opportunity to end it all, Lorraine must have pulled the clip off the pen and succumbed to the temptation to escape this purgatory.

Over these past few hellish days, Eve had implored Lorraine to try and hold it together for the sake of her husband and child. Eve knew Lorraine was not as mentally tough as herself; Lorraine had confided in Eve that she had been on anti-depressants for a long time after the birth of her one and only child. But Eve had not expected her to give up so easily. As she had told Lorraine over and over again, it was surely a good sign that their abductors hadn't finished them off. The longer they remained alive, watered and fed and led to the loo every two hours, the less likely it seemed that their kidnappers intended killing them. The presence of an oil heater that clicked on intermittently told Eve it was not in the kidnappers' interests that they should die of hypothermia in the freezing cold, damp outhouse.

There was nothing to do but holler; sure she would get a beating for her troubles, but Lorraine was going to slip away very soon if she, Eve, didn't sound the alarm. Eve took a swig of the cheap and nasty orange squash to moisten her dry throat then began to yell.

It felt like she'd been screaming forever before she heard a key turn in the door. Eve screwed her eyes as the piercing sunlight streamed through the door. Britney Skinner let out a string of expletives, as her nasty little eyes took in the sight of Lorraine Girding drenched in blood.

"I know some basic First Aid," Eve told her in a voice hoarse from screaming. "If you undo me, I can stop the bleeding. I think she's still breathing."

Skinner squatted down in front of the limp woman and held her palm in front of Lorraine's mouth.

"She's still alive," Skinner noted. It cheered Eve somewhat to hear the relief in Skinner's tone.

"Look, if you at least just slacken my ropes so that I can reach her, I can stop her bleeding. She'll survive if we can just stop the blood! Please!" Eve Beckford stared imploringly at the ugly twenty-something woman before her.

Skinner grunted in disgust, clearly in a quandary.

"Look, you stupid cow," Beckford exclaimed, fury rising from within. "You need to fetch some bandages, or tea-towels if you don't have any, or even rip some of her clothes. You need to tie strips tightly around her wrists. She's no use to you dead, is she? Where will the drug money come from then?"

"Shut-up, you stupid bitch," a clearly panicking Britney Skinner yelled. She slapped Beckford hard across the cheek and booted her in the midriff.

Beckford doubled over, insofar as she could with the rope restraints on. Skinner then disappeared back to the house to reappear a moment later with some scissors and a bag of j-cloths. She proceeded to cut several of the blue cloths lengthways to form ties which she secured around Lorraine Girding's wrists with a knot.

"Just you shut up, or you'll be the one bleeding next time, lady," Skinner hissed before leaving the two women in near darkness again.

Eve looked across at Lorraine Girding once more. The bleeding appeared to have stopped, but was it too late?

42

Armed with a recent photo of Britney Skinner obtained from her mother, Parlour took to the pubs in and around the ferry ports. He drew a blank each time, with nobody able to recognise Skinner from the photo or recollect seeing her with a lanky spotty youth with bleached blonde hair.

The rest of the team were also experiencing little joy in the hunt for Britney Skinner. There was no way a televised appeal could be made for information leading to the whereabouts of Britney Skinner, as there was no evidence she was indeed the abductor of Lorraine Girding, Eve Beckford and Juliet Parlour. There was nothing to be done but carry on pounding the streets, thrusting the photo of Britney Skinner under the noses of the public, in the vain hope someone somewhere had caught sight of this nasty woman since the morning of Wednesday 16 November.

Parlour was finding it hard work going from pub to pub at lunchtime, watching Christmas shoppers tuck into platters of succulent pub grub, while he was very much on the job. It was so tempting to take an hour out to fill his stomach, but unlike Detective Alan Banks in his favourite detective novels, Parlour found a heavy lunch was not conducive to good sleuthing. He would need to be at his razor-sharp best to nail the abductor of these unfortunate women.

So reluctantly procuring a floppy sandwich and a bottle of orange juice from a local newsagent, Parlour returned to his car for a quick bite to eat. It was a crisp, sunny, late autumnal day and the Christmas shoppers were out in force, with cars queuing bumper to bumper on all roads into Portsmouth City Centre. Whatever had become of the Day of Rest?

Despite the gravity of the case he was working on, Parlour felt curiously elated. Perhaps it was the unexpected sunshine, perhaps it was just sheer relief at having *his* wife, at least, back safe and well – whatever it was, Parlour felt at one with himself and his Maker that sunny Sunday afternoon. He flicked on the car stereo and tuned into a local station that he knew played 60s gold all day long at the weekend.

Parlour turned up the familiar sound of the Beatles, whose existence itself, in his view, was reason enough to sing praises to God on the Sabbath. As the words to the song poured from the car speaker, Parlour suddenly felt a strange tingling in his scalp.

Of course! Why on earth hadn't he thought of that before?

Stuffing the remnants of his sandwich back into the cellophane pocket, Parlour turned the key in the ignition and grabbed the portable siren from the glove compartment. He slapped it on the roof of his Mercedes SLK and started up the wailing lament. He would need to exercise some muscle to beat the traffic.

43

"Lord, just let this be right!" Parlour muttered to himself as he weaved in and out the busy traffic, enjoying the power the flashing blue light gave him despite his anxiety.

Within five minutes, he had pulled up right outside the Island-link terminal at Portsmouth Harbour. Shoving his Hampshire Constabulary notice on the dashboard to prevent an overzealous parking attendant from clamping his unmarked car, Parlour dashed into the office. Flashing his police ID, he pushed through the queues to the front desk.

Within minutes he had the information he wanted from the Wightlink Duty Manager. A tall, blond youth with acne by the name of Richie Blake was indeed employed by Island-link, based at Portsmouth Harbour, though that day he was working at the Ryde Pierhead terminal. Arranging for a member of the Island force to pick him up the other side, Parlour boarded the next available FastCat for the 18 minute journey to Ryde. He would bring in the team at Billock CID the moment his suspicions were confirmed.

Parlour found a seat and clenched his fists tensely as "the cat" sped through the Solent to the Isle of Wight, living up to its name that Tuesday as the nation's sunniest outpost.

As Parlour disembarked, the first face he saw was the acne-bedevilled one of Richie Blake, manning the security gate, behind which stood a line of passengers waiting to make the journey back to the mainland. His heart thumped and his scalp tingled again. Was this the bosom buddy of Britney Skinner, or had he been chasing wild geese?

Parlour left the harbour area and soon located PC Tom Biggin of Isle of Wight Police. Within minutes another employee had been found to person the security barrier and a jumpy looking Richie Blake sat in the back of a squad car.

"Recognise this woman?" Parlour enquired, thrusting the close-up of Britney Skinner in his face. It was enough to make any man shrink, but Blake sat impassive. Parlour knew in a nano-second that he recognised Skinner.

"We have a witness to say that you are good pals - very good pals - with Miss Skinner," Parlour informed him.

Blake said nothing.

"If you like, I can go and enquire at your place of work. I'm sure they must have seen you together. I can fetch the CCTV tapes and check them out... though I expect you've removed them, haven't you?"

"What *are* you on about?" Blake sneered, wiping his nose on the back of his hand. Parlour winced; he really was quite an unpleasant young man. It was no wonder overseas tourists expressed displeasure at the standard of customer services in the UK, with greasy monosyllabic toe-rags like this interfacing with the public.

"Do you want to tell us now, or do you want the whole island to see you being driven to the station in a squad car?" PC Biggin enquired.

"I don't know no Britney Skinner," Blake grunted.

"Who mentioned her name was Britney?" Parlour enquired smoothly.

Thick as well as rude, he thought to himself. Blake cursed and Parlour knew he had him over a barrel.

"So what's your cut, then?" Parlour persisted. "Ten k? Twenty k? Or has she got you on the cheap? Blab and I'll grass on your role in all this?"

"I'm saying nothing," Blake muttered.

"Then you're a very silly boy," Biggin informed him. "Because Miss Skinner's in a lot of trouble – a whole hot tubful of it – and the less you co-operate, the longer your custodial sentence. And believe you me, you don't want to end up in Parkhurst!"

"Let me guess," Parlour said smoothly. "Your role is to meet and greet the boneheads with the white van at Portsmouth Harbour. You accompany our poor drugged lady in the wheelchair onto the cat, no questions asked because you work here. Then it's conveniently your lunchbreak which gives you an hour to take the woman to your grubby little lock-up and chain her up, just before the sedative wears off. Am I right so far?"

"It's a workshop," Blake mumbled, knowing the game was up.

"Where's the farm, Richie?" Parlour asked in a steely tone of voice that belied his puny stature.

"About half an hour away," Blake replied. "On the Sandown road. It belonged to my Grandad. He passed on and left it to my parents. They can't afford to run it; it's up for sale, they've sold the livestock and the machinery. It's lying empty at the moment. That's where Brit is hiding the women."

"Why?" Parlour wondered, as Biggins radioed for help from the local force.

Blake shrugged. "Don't really know. It's not about the money, not really. You'd have to ask Brit. She's mental. I was just..."

"Being a mate?" Parlour asked sarcastically.

"I needed the dosh," Blake conceded. "I took a neighbour's car out for a spin and... um... spun it out of control. My parents sorted it with them, but I wasn't insured and that, so..."

"So their insurance won't pay up?" Parlour guessed, shaking his head in wonder at the young man's crass stupidity. His parents, who were decent people, by the sounds of it, would have rather done without the money, he was sure of it, than have their son an accessory to such a serious crime.

In less than thirty minutes, they had pulled up outside Brindle Farm. Half a dozen or so squad cars were already parked outside, and Parlour could see that some uniformed officers had already encircled a pebble-dashed outbuilding to the rear of the boarded-up farmhouse.

Sergeant John Innes of IOW police approached Parlour, who had left the cuffed Richie Blake in the car.

"The women are in the outbuilding all right. One of them is fighting for her life – she's gone and slashed her wrists. They've been bound, but she's lost a lot of blood, Sir. We've radioed for an ambulance. But unfortunately, Miss Skinner is also in there with them. She's got a ruddy great kitchen knife on her and says she's going to slit the throats of both women if we don't vacate the premises now. We have an officer at the window on the side of the workshop. Skinner's crouched down beside the women."

He approached the building. "Miss Skinner – this is Detective Chief Inspector Mark Parlour of Billock CID on the mainland. You need to put that knife down right now if you don't want to spend the rest of your life in prison."

Skinner retorted with an expletive.

"Come on," Parlour chided her. "You know there's no issue of us leaving the property so you may as well quit now and make life a little better for yourself."

Parlour met with a torrent of vile abuse this time. Time to try a different tack.

"Miss Skinner – Britney – I know why you're so angry with these women. I know your family story, I understand how mad these women must make you, but this has got to stop now. This is insane, and you know it."

Where was a skilled negotiator when you needed one, Parlour wondered, rueing his relative ineptness at the task in hand. "Britney, put that knife down now and I promise you, you will significantly reduce the chances of a long custodial sentence. Think of your mother. Does she deserve this? Can you imagine what it would do to her, to lose you?"

Parlour struck a chord with that one.

"She's welling up, boss," the officer window-side informed Parlour over the radio.

"Put down the knife now, Britney," Parlour instructed. He heard the sound of metal clang on the hard concrete floor and stood back for the armoured officers to smash the door down.

Head down, Britney Skinner was handcuffed and led to a secure police van. Parlour dashed to the two hostages and drawing a penknife from his pocket, slit the ropes around both women's ankles and wrists. Eve Beckford was helped to her feet by Biggins and taken out to the first of two Isle of Wight ambulances that had just pulled up.

Parlour laid an ear to Lorraine Girding's chest.

"Is she breathing, Sir?" Biggins enquired, returning to the garage.

Parlour shook his head slowly. "I don't think so."

He felt his own heart thump against his chest wall as he lifted her head to touch her cheek. "She's cold."

He pressed a finger against the pulse in her neck but there was nothing...

or....

Parlour stood back to let the paramedics attend to her. "I think I just felt a pulse in her neck," he told them nervously.

"Stand back, please, Sir," a female paramedic instructed. Parlour left them to their job, hands clenched tightly into fists, willing Lorraine Girding to be still alive.

An exclamation of "Got it" in what seemed like an age later, told Parlour all he needed to know. Sinking to his haunches in relief, he exhaled an almighty sigh of thanksgiving as an oxygen mask was attached to Lorraine Girding and she was wheeled into a second waiting ambulance.

Parlour found a spot outside where he could get a reception and dialled Adam Beckford followed by Robert Girding. The calls back to base could wait another ten minutes. The safety of the two women and some much needed solace for their husbands and children, were top priority at that precise moment.

44

Later that day, with reports duly written up and husbands reunited with wives, Parlour poured himself a large glass of red wine and sat back in his favourite leather recliner. He shut his eyes and congratulated himself on a job well done – eventually. At least he'd got to Lorraine Girding in the nick of time. She'd be kept in overnight in the private wing of Billock General; she had lost a great deal of blood and a trained eye would need to be kept on her. Once back at home, Mrs Girding would be referred to a counsellor who would help her talk through and come to terms with her terrible ordeal. The counsellor would also discuss Mrs Girding's general mental health and recommend she be prescribed anti-depressive medication once more if need be.

After a thorough check-up at the same hospital, Eve Beckford had been allowed to return home to her husband. The children would remain at her mother's house in Kent until she had fully recovered from her ordeal. Mrs Beckford would recover much faster, having been locked up for a shorter period of time, and being altogether more resilient.

Juliet had fully recovered from her brief abduction and was now keen to work out just how Parlour had gone from zero to hero in the space of an hour earlier that day. Lowering Rowan into his playpen, Juliet poured herself a glass of her favourite blueberry and pomegranate juice and sat cross legged on the sofa opposite her husband.

"So do you think The Sausage has forgiven you yet?" Juliet grinned.

Superintendent Dewhurst had been initially furious with Parlour for dashing off to the Island on his own and not involving the rest of the team in the arrest of Britney Skinner and Richie Blake. However, Parlour was sure that when Dewhurst calmed down and realised they'd saved the life of Lorraine Girding by the skin of their teeth, he would forgive

Parlour the adrenalin rush. The paramedic had told them that Lorraine was so weak, they had barely been able to register her pulse on an initial examination of her in the dank farm outbuilding.

"What'll happen to Britney Skinner, d'you reckon?" Juliet wondered.

"She'll get a custodial sentence – five to ten years I'd say. She's agreed to return the money, which she'd barely dipped into. And she did save Mrs Girding's life by bandaging her wrists with those j-cloths. The judge will take that into account."

"What possessed her to do such a terrible thing, though? Sheer jealousy?"

Parlour nodded. "She really suffered when her parents split up. She lost her father, their nice house, and all the security they had known. She was forced to move to a grotty little flat and live on cheap nasty food and charity shop clothes. That's what precipitated the plan to abduct the Yummy Mummies she saw come into the supermarket week in week out. In her previous role as a delivery driver, she'd visit their houses and see how they lived. It made her blood boil; it all seemed so unfair to her. She became consumed with bitterness and rage and decided she wanted some of what they had. A couple of hundred k would provide her with a hefty deposit on a smart house, probably abroad. It was never about drugs. We also found the remains of the scrambler motorbike one of the abductors used to grab the ransom money from Fryer's Dip. It had been dismembered and placed in crates inside the transit."

"The transit was at the farm on the Island?"

Parlour nodded. "We found it in a barn."

"What'll happen to the two men?"

"Once they've been picked up – and Denton's following up some leads as I speak - they'll be put away for a while, too."

"But you know who they are?"

Parlour nodded. "We found a North Harbour KFC receipt in the glove compartment. It was dated a few weeks back. We got hold of the CCTV footage for the relevant time of day and found an image of them walking back to the white van. We had a stroke of luck - one of the KFC employees went to school with the driver of the van and identified him for us. We then found a neighbour of Kevin Schooner – that's his name – who told us they were heading up north to some mates in Leeds. So several squad cars are tearing up the M1 as I speak! We've also got a team searching for Britney Skinner's cousin Kyle. He's our mystery computer hacker – Kyle Entwhistle used to work on the website of a leading rival of BestCo, so he would be fully conversant with online grocery systems. Mrs Skinner dumped him in it, trying to save her daughter's bacon."

"That's a lot of bacon," Juliet smirked, betraying a distinct lack of body-awareness. Her own BMI was creeping up the scale on a daily basis.

"Richie Blake should get off more lightly," Parlour continued, "but he'll still be looking at a custodial sentence, as will our friend Mr Jankowicz. They were both in on the abductions."

"Kat's husband? I thought you said they had nothing to do with all of this?"

"Skinner slipped him fifty quid to spy out of his fifteenth floor window and inform her when the ransom had been placed in Fryer's Dip."

Juliet frowned. "I don't get it – what connection would Kat's husband have with Britney Skinner?"

"Grygor hangs around with some pretty undesirable types – I guess someone who knows Britney also knew that Jankowicz lived in the high-rise overlooking the dip and would be able to keep look-out for her. We did wonder why there was a pair of binoculars in his room – we assumed it was purely for spying on young totty, given his penchant for teenage girls."

"Do you think his wife was aware of this?"

"I think she had her doubts about him," Parlour confirmed. "I expect she agreed to keep schtum about his extra-curricular activities, so to speak, if he gave her an alibi for her alleged trip out to the pub with her mate. We know she was meeting our greasy little Estate Agent friend – I don't expect for one minute she told him the full truth. I expect they had some kind of mutual agreement not to delve too far into each other's private business. Not the healthiest of marriages, that one."

"So glad we don't have any secrets, Mark," Juliet said with feeling. "Well, apart from my one and only online grocery delivery."

I wish that was the only secret, Parlour thought guiltily to himself, his expression clouding for an instant. Maybe he would tell her one day about his near cock-up, but Karen was right. They had both been in a bad place mentally; it was a fleeting moment in time best put down to experience and left firmly in the past. He knew he could trust Karen Preece to be discreet; it was one of her professional qualities Parlour so valued. Karen had never displayed anything but the utmost loyalty to him.

"I still haven't found out how you worked out that the women were on the Island," Juliet frowned, oblivious to Parlour's momentary discomfort.

Parlour grinned. "It was quite sublime. I'd walked for miles, going in and out of shops and pubs flashing the photo of Skinner at everyone. I was getting nowhere. I was so hacked off, I decided I would grab some lunch and go sit in the car for a while. Just sitting there in the sun, I suddenly felt all happy and grateful to be alive. I turned on the radio, thought I'd listen to that 60s Gold programme on Southern City Radio. And would you believe it, what should come on but *Ticket to Ride*! It just suddenly clicked... the van heading towards Portsmouth, talk of a "cat", a holding place with British sockets. I realised the women hadn't been taken by ferry to France, they'd gone by catamaran to the Isle of Wight – Ryde to be precise."

"That's total genius, Mark," Juliet said admiringly, "and more than a touch jammy."

"I hazarded a guess that the spotty blonde youth that Britney has been seen hanging out with had some kind of job with Island-link. How else would they be able to transport a drugged up woman in a wheelchair without anyone asking awkward questions? The bonehead guys obviously drove the women to the terminal, shoved them in a wheelchair, and Richie Blake took care of the rest – for a cut in the profits, naturally."

"What was she going to do with the women, though? She couldn't have kept them there indefinitely. The hunt would have extended to the Island eventually, surely?"

"I think she planned to abduct another two or three ladies - yourself and a few more who fitted her person spec. Once she had the readies, she'd have released the women in the middle of nowhere and disappeared, changing her name again. We'd have caught up with her in the end, though. She wasn't as clever as she thought she was."

"No match for you, that's for sure," Juliet smiled, immensely proud of her husband. "The Sausage must be so gutted you worked it out before him."

"I think I have to give someone else the credit, really," Parlour protested. "It just has to be divine intervention that the Beatles came on the radio at that moment."

"You still reacted as you did," Juliet said loyally. "So what now, Detective Chief Superintendent Parlour?"

Parlour chuckled. "I tell you what's now – a thumping good holiday with my wife and son. One thing the past week has taught me is that you can't put a price on the life of those closest to you. I just want to relax and enjoy the two of you properly. I've been on the internet and you can get some bargain deals this time of year –so long as we avoid Christmas and New Year. What do you say to a month or two down under?"

"Remember what happened last time we went to Oz?" Juliet grinned, recollecting their wonderful honeymoon to the West Coast of Australia.

"We nearly didn't come back!" Parlour chuckled, recalling the flat with an ocean view that they had fallen in love with. "So what do you say, Mrs Parlour?"

"I say let's do it," Juliet grinned.

On a one-way ticket, Parlour thought to himself, far from in jest.

About the author

Carol A Shepherd is an author, college lecturer and LGBT faith activist from Eastleigh, near Southampton, UK. You can find her books at www.carolshepherdbooks.info

If you valued this book, the author would greatly appreciate a review on Amazon to spread the word and support independent publishers.

You can also subscribe to Carol's newsletter, The Bi Christian Writer and claim a free novella:
https://www.subscribepage.com/bichristianwriter

More titles from Easy Yoke Publishing can be found at www.easyyoke.org

Also in the series:

Death by Peanuts (Parlour Mystery 1)
The Allotment Affair (Parlour Mystery 2)

By the same author....

Death by Peanuts

Who could have anticipated the sudden death of a church warden from the designer village of Deverton? DI Mark Parlour can scarcely believe his eyes when he finds ex-serviceman, Terence Haynes, slumped across a plate of éclairs on picking his wife up from a church meeting. It soon becomes clear that this was murder – and one which could only have been carried out by a member of the Church Council in attendance that day!

"The reason for the murder was outstandingly brilliant and very credible. This alone puts it right up amongst the best of domestic crime stories I have read (and there are lots!). The humour is first class and should appeal to many."

OV, W Glamorgan

"For once a crime book that doesn't rely on shock value or unpleasant anatomical details to provide interest! The plot is well worked out and the story moves forward nicely."

JW, W Sussex

"Absolutely brilliant! I couldn't put it down. Really funny and kept me guessing until the end."

JR, Hampshire